The Meridian Protocol

A NOVEL

HAMON DE QUILLAN

GLOBAL EAST-WEST. LONDON

Contents

Part One

THE EUROPEAN OUTAGE

Chapter One

The Dark Heart of Paris

Paris, 2:00 AM

An unplanned blackout swept through the City, and Nova Li absorbed the strange scene from the balcony of her corner penthouse. Street lamps and tower lights had gone dark, leaving the skyline a puzzle of black and rust, cut and pasted by the curt flicker of backup strobes. Night had always dimmed Paris, but tonight the dark felt directed, even levelled. From a floor above the baguettes and bitters, she heard a muted tide of voices, muted sirens, and the soft thump of misplaced bicycle bells trying to carry their riders home.

Protocols she had never memorised fired on her screen, and the refusal of panic only sharpened her focus. She had turned the City and the world inside-out a thousand times, yet the symmetry of this ordered ruin surprised her. Phasing blackouts in district eleven, the opera hive, and beside the City—everyone selected like a hearing imprint but never a signature. Watchful rather than worried, she traced the luminous path of the backup mosaic. In the half of the City that still breathed, she saw the standard grammar of alert, alarm, and the calm that follows calculation.

Night smeared itself over Paris like spilt ink, quiet except for the faint moan of police sirens. Usually, the City hummed through the small hours, but now it wore a hood of dread. A power cut was rarely innocent—Nova felt it, a warning that murmured for attention. A catalogue of dark scenarios marched through her head, catalogued by years spent studying shifting borders and hidden nets of power.

The moment stretched away from her deliberate breath, and her private comm unit chirped with the familiar, predatory buzz. The signal was thick with layers, sender erased, and the scraps it gave—coordinates, ciphered keywords, the name of a paper mill—pointed upward, mapping a bigger, bloodier design. Her pulse quickened with the promise of each new fragment, but dread lagged a heartbeat behind.

As the silence, the unknown, and the weight of her own responsibility mingled, Nova Li came to a stark realisation: France was the stage, and she, an unwelcome cast member. With each breath, the spectre of failure loomed larger, too bright to allow for a second chance. Transitioning from a mere observer to a predator, she began to unravel the first lock of the mystery. The dark expanse of Paris now lay beneath her, a web of possibilities. With a determined step, she embraced the shadows that pulsed within the heart of the City.

The City lay wrapped in the hush before dawn, streetlamps spilling pale light that stretched out like ghost fingers over the uneven stones. Nova leaned on the cold wrought-iron rail of the old bridge and stared down the basin of the Seine, the tiny stars of the Eiffel Tower mirrored on the water like sparks from a dying fire. They always pulled her, those little lights, but tonight they smiled with a secret she could almost taste. Memories rippled through her like the river itself, one then another, and with each came the quickening of her heart. Paris had always whispered to her, fierce and tender, but the whisper had sharpened, edged with the hush of coming storm. A chill slid under her collar, heavier than the dawn. The truths she had buried pressed against her ribs, sharp and rusted, and she could feel the tiny seams of her life beginning to split. A single, terrible choice glimmered in the distance, the one that once unfixed would spin her life like coins off a slate. Lagos came tumbling back in that instant, the City where the first impossible thread had shown itself. Kofi's voice, low and fractured, echoed in her ear: "Know the answers and you will be alone." And still, she had followed the light, hour by hour, step by step, each footfall a promise she could now hardly recall.

Yet pieces still floated beyond her reach, a riddle that refused to display its proper shape. Paris. Lagos. Buenos Aires. Singapore. The very names vibrated in her mind, almost humming, as if the four cities were knotted by threads no one else could see. Each held a shard of the puzzle that had wrapped itself around her, and she could not turn away. How had her ordinary life caught the attention of powers she could barely name? The pulse of the mission—steady, unrelenting—beat in her ears and pushed her forward into the black. Determination shone in her gaze, twin flares that ignited the stillness, and she silently swore to drag the hidden truth into the light, no matter the cost. She understood that her part in this silent play was no accident, no stray coin on the street; it was a choice she could not dodge. Spine straight, she pulled the night air into her lungs, letting the chill sting and steady her. The path of trap and whisper that lay before her was fresh and unmarked. Nova stepped forward, ready to greet the shadows that throbbed in the very lungs of Paris.

Lagos, 8:00 AM

Early morning mist trailed the Lagos streets like ghost fingers, giving the City an eerie hush. When the reddish sun lifted, the metropolis exploded into life, its pulse like a war drum calling the living. Creaks of motorbikes, shouts, and the ever-present whistle of hawkers glued to bread and pure-water sachets filled every narrow lane and too-small market. In the leaping noise, Kofi moved as if the world had stilled for him alone. A veteran of secrets and shadows, he walked the crooked streets like a hyena trailing a wounded buck, thin shoulders curling into the traffic, thick boots whispering. His gaze, sharper than the trade-blades sold under tarpaulin, darted from tired market-women to amused kids to idle Okada-drivers, reading every lifted brow and sudden smile for poison. The day had found him, and nothing alive would turn him aside. His prey hid somewhere in the night-drenched City, a ghost like a slipped card, whose next move could shatter the truce stitched hard across the dusty maps of West Africa. The deeper Kofi pressed into Lagos, the more the City's breath entered his own. Colonial chains, gunfire in the streets, the roar of independence—every shudder and cry, every brick and burnt folktale, pressed on his back like a grudging ancestor reminding him why he kept walking forward.

Behind the bright lights and hurry of Lagos, shadowy streets waited—streets humming with whispered deals, shady compacts, and secrets darker than midnight. Kofi felt the warning sigh of danger in his spine, but every footfall pushed him deeper. Each breath drew the puzzle tighter, the puzzle that hung over the region like storm clouds. Surging crowds, steamy air, and the City's heartbeat raised the hair on his neck. In Lagos, yesterday and today twisted around each other, tossing up puzzles that snared anyone with curious blood. When the sun hammered straight overhead, Kofi stood upon the crack in the hour past dropped behind him, future blazing ahead. The ground beneath his feet felt thin, like the edge of a knife, but his attitude filled the air with promise. The chapter before him glimmered with trial, with shaken truths, and with the quiet chance to steer a whole nation toward dawn or further into tempests.

Buenos Aires, 9:00 PM

The night pulsed with the heartbeat of the City. Starved of breeze, the humid air clung to the marble façades like perfume, and the flat, aching notes of a guitar floated from a moonlit plaza. In a silent pocket between neon signs, a lone figure caught the wavering lamplight and slipped between shadows. Jorge Córdoba, the ghost you never mention, moved through narrow streets the way a wine-dark river cuts through stone. He was already a legend—his boardrooms chilled by whispers of failure, his ledger inked in overturned reputations. When his silhouette crossed the threshold of the Mirador, velvet and polished brass, time itself stilled. Guests paused, forks raised; in one measured gesture, Jorge commanded the night and locked the future. Tailored midnight cloth hugged his shoulders; his eyes were hollow lanterns. At a table with impossible privacy, he joined others equally masked—wealth, power, and silence sitting shoulder to shoulder. Their words wove dangerously close, a blueprint for continents. Invisible to the conspirators, a small team of cameras and tempered nerves danced in the rafters, cataloguing the poison before it was poured.

Across the other end of Buenos Aires, restless journalist Maria del Carmen huddled over her desk, the hushed clang of her typewriter like the ticking of a countdown. She had moulded gossip, shadows, and strained photos into a map whose crossroads warned her that the global scandal she'd been chasing was no longer fake smoke. Before she tasted the morning coffee that might dull her nerves, she had already written two obituaries for herself. The moon rode high when she slid her latest column through the slot of the City's quietest revista; the letters, one last bridge, called strangers, lovers, and enemies into the same clearing. One by one, the stories grew hungry for blood, and the City, dangling over dark water, began to knit a single, ruthless shoreline. The same rooftops that once cradled cathedral bells now masked no fewer than twelve listening posts; the same belligerent breeze that stirred the milongas now dried her palms for the next blood-dipped step. The cigar smoke at Morales's bar tasted less of leaf and more of data, and every face in the shadows was teaching her a new consonant in the language of terror. Beneath the sequined glamour that trickled from Recoleta's ballrooms, other gamblers stacked currencies of innocence and betrayal; under their whispered tango, a gasp of steel entertained no sentiment. Destiny, it seemed, had sewn a single thread through polished cigar cases, bruised hearts, and blatant lies. That thread, alive and final, now yanked every one of them toward the awakening dawn, where courage would step off the curb and into the headlights of a train that did not brake.

Singapore, 3:00 PM

The City buzzed like a high-voltage circuit, the sun hanging overhead like a molten coin, gilding the glass-and-steel spires that shot from the ground. In her jewel-box penthouse high above the clamour, Nova drummed her fingertips on a marble slab, the beat steady as clockwork. Before her, the City fanned out, a holotape of luminous arteries, each line a hidden gain, each curve a lurking danger. She was at home here, where ambition sold both lightning and velvet, and the crack of a deal was as shocking as the clang of a dropped coin. Leaning back, the ghost of a private grin crossed her face, a spark of victory anticipated rather than claimed. In Singapore, pacts and betrayals exchanged places faster than a breath, and Nova meant to collect the scalp of every gambler that crossed her path. Her gaze roamed the skyline, scanning like a hawk, waiting for the telltale flicker that meant the right door had just opened and a chance for the next leap had just been priced.

The City buzzed like a million wings in the late sun, and its rhythm sank into Nova's blood, quickening the beat of her own bold plans. Light washed over the rooftops in a river of gold, and each shimmer drove her steps toward the midnight pulse of Paris, where fate and hunger would finally crash against each other. She could not yet see the ripples her resolve would send over the oceans; the girl who left would not be the woman who returned. Standing in the smooth chill of the penthouse, she whispered the promise in her own heartbeat: seize the edge, topple the barrier, climb higher than the sky. Tomorrow would not be a siding—it would be her throne.

The humid air of Singapore felt electric as Nova walked through the crowded streets. She had always played the game with care, measuring each step, but the prize tonight was too large for caution. All the training, all the nights spent watching, had built her for this single heist. Months spent with the City's elite—handing out the right compliments at the right openings—had kept her cover solid as diamond. Now, the chandeliers of the Raffles Hotel glittered above her like stars she could pluck for herself. Nova stepped into the ballroom, knowing a slip would mean the end. She could hear the ticking of every second, every link of the plan falling into line, or out of it.

Across the hall, she spotted the man—wealthy, shadowed by titans, anchored to secrets Nova needed like air. The room pulsed blue with cigar smoke and orchestral notes. Nova slipped through it like a sip of strong tea, all smile and easy laugh. The right words landed like butterfly kisses, and soon he was leaning close, palm pressed to the cool marble of a pillar. The noise faded, the lights dimmed, and it was just her and the diamond. She could feel the moment's heartbeat pulsing in the space between them, louder than music, more audible than hesitations. The plan had led her here. Now, the plan would live or die by one final heartbeat.

With a snap-of-the-fingers grace, she traded the businessman's ID card for a dummy that could pass for the real deal, sealing her ticket to the data she was after.

Once she stepped away, Nova's pulse kicked like a racehorse. Part one had run like a charm, but the clock was already ticking. Keeping her movements smooth, she threaded her way through the sea of suits, the room a blur of chatter and clinking glasses.

When she slipped through the final doorway and the balmy Singapore air hugged her body, she quickened her pace. The meeting spot sat a few blocks down, and her partner's ride had to be waiting. Once inside, the thrill of the last-minute heist crashed over her like a wave. The real grind was coming, but the glittering skyline ahead, spangled like a million promise stars, told her she was steeled for it. Grinning, she signalled her partner, and the engine growled low. The City swallowed them in shadow, already cradling the quiet rumours of their nighttime game.

The Lagos street shimmered under a morning sun that spilt liquid gold everywhere Kofi Adewale walked. The market roared around him—haggling voices, the clang of scales, the teasing scent of suya—but Kofi heard a different music. As an intelligence officer, he had learned that safety often whispered, while danger screamed. He had spent years trusting that faintest of whispers. Today, his instincts pointed him toward a corner stall that shouldn't be there. Instead of beans or batik or the usual morning scents, the stall heaved with jagged circuit boards, empty housings, and bags of chips that seemed to shift and shimmer like living things. The stall keeper, a quiet man with the colour of worn leather, kept wiping his palms and scanning the street as though the street itself had a pulse he was afraid of. Kofi slowed his heartbeat. He focused his eyes and let the market blur. After a minute, he walked close as if to ask the price of a resistor—then let the question slide sideways. He complimented the man on his rare stock and mother-tongued the compliment heavily. The keeper ducked his gaze, answered with missing data, and Kofi felt the rip of a lie in the dry air. Kofi shrugged and moved on, but his mind pressed the stall and the vendor onto a growing map of worry. Something whispered underneath the market's roar, and Kofi was no longer sure he could ignore it.

Kofi felt the weight of the new puzzle settle on his shoulders the instant he crossed the precinct gate, its eerie quiet now amplifying his pulse. This was no petty crime; no, this shadow slid well past Lagos and slipped beneath every border, tightening like a noose around the entire globe. Pulling his shoulders back, he entered his cluttered office. He flipped on the single flickering bulb, anxious to sweep the desk clean of yesterday's papers and lay out the jagged facts that buzzed in his head like angry wasps. Word on the street, an untraceable drone, a disappeared whistle-blower, and now the cargo seal on a Lagos cargo hold snapped clean as a broken promise. Kofi arranged the tidbits in hesitant rows, his hands steadying to the rhythm of a single conviction: the darkness of this conspiracy would not outlive his light. What he could not yet imagine, and would soon discover to his cost, was that every answer he unearthed would uncoil a darker riddle, pulling him deeper into a maze where intellect would be his only shield and his unyielding integrity the cruellest test.

Elena had built her career on gut instinct and quick think-ing. These qualities wore as comfortably as her favourite leather jacket. Now, holed up in a quiet Buenos Aires café with rain streaking the window, a small, cold knot twisted in her stomach. Kofi had looked at her in the corridor earlier that week, eyebrows raised, and the look had gnawed at her like a loose tooth. It meant he'd found a piece of the operation he couldn't account for, and that was never a good sign.

The coffee cup in her hands was lukewarm and sour, but the taste was the least of her worries. The inner voice that had kept her alive in three countries warned her that the next hour would tip the balance and, for once, the voice sounded alarmed. She checked the small screen of her digi-tal watch—nothing flashy, just a habit. The hands ticked like a countdown. This wasn't a training exercise anymore; too many lives hung in the balance of the move she would make next.

Elena stood up straight and set her jaw, the burning need

to know driving her forward. Outside, Buenos Aires rolled out ahead like an open question, the streets alive with both promise and peril. She wrapped her coat tighter, the night air biting her skin like a warning that the darkness never forgot to watch back.

She slipped through the swirl of pedestrians and cars, feet finding the rhythm of the City she had walked a thousand times. Her breath kept a secret count of nerves as she drank in every passing look, every hurried step. To the world, she was a ghost. Still, to her, every stranger was an unopened envelope and every narrow lane an invitation to something buried.

The trail narrowed at last to a narrow shop, a fading sign fighting a last stand of gilt against the soot of the years. Between two flat-faced buildings, it sat like a locked diary, its windows dressed in pale lace that had almost forgotten daylight. Elena nudged the warped door, and a long sigh of hinges answered; the tiny bell overhead rang a note that was both welcome and warning.

The shop smelled like old paper and old wood and maybe a little like faded dreams. Sunlight spilt in collarbone-sky beams, making dust dance like memory, and every shelf seemed to lean in, waiting. Elena roamed the narrow aisles, her fingers grazing metal and glass, and felt the same chill the hush between raindrops brings. Someone—or some-thing—was watching her, a shadow stitching her every heartbeat for a pocket in the past.

Then, between a brass telescope and a moth-smooth box, she saw it: a journal, the colour of storm-muffled leather, pushed high and lonely like a secret the rafters kept. She felt the pages hum at the edge of her blood. When she reached, her fingers tingled against the brittle spine, and she felt the first of many brittle whispers. The pages were a pale yellow, almost the colour of first light on frost, and the angles of her breath made them turn too fast, skipping riddles that made her blood vibrate.

Footsteps cracked the hush, louder than her heartbeat, and she folded the journal inside her coat like a moth folding her wings. The shopkeeper appeared, a doorway of quiet himself. She kept her face plain, her heart a dark sky, and for a heartbeat their eyes wove the same strange thread: curiosity and warning and maybe a touch of kindness. In that thread, she felt the journal pull her forward, deeper into the ravel of lies and old clocks and untold stories that made her City breathe.

Omar cradled his cooled coffee cup in the shadowy café, watching Paris pulse through the rain-streaked window. He loved the City's restless heartbeat, yet tonight a greater drumbeat thrummed behind his ribs. He stole a glance at his watch, the small glowing circle reminding him that the hour had come. A silhouette broke through the haze of mist and neon, then crossed the glass and strode toward his small table. It was Kofi, his closest ally, the once-loose jacket now buttoned tight, the fierceness in his eyes sharpened. Kofi sank down, clasped his hands, and after a taut breath leaned nearer than custom allowed. 'I found the channel,' he said, voice so low only the dark eavesdropper ghosts could catch it. 'But the channel's keeper demands a price. A heavy one.' Omar felt the floor under him bend; the intel they craved had the power to tilt the world, yet the offering it craved tasted bitter on the tongue. Kofi let a silence settle, then added, 'I've turned the coin in my head a hundred ways. The gain outweighs the cut, but only if we keep our feet light and our pockets ready.' Omar inhaled, mind now a speeding train through circuits of what-ifs and maybe-then. He understood the balance Kofi had laid before him, and he felt the delicate fulcrum already shifting.

Sitting in the Paris café, the idea felt like standing on thin ice, ready to crack. Outside the flashing neon of the street, Nova's name buzzed in the back of each mind like an old radio. Omar stared into his espresso cup, clouds of steam mixing with the autumn air, and promised himself—for keeps—that he'd carry the load, whatever the load cost. He didn't see, in the curve of that small moment, the future beginning to spin in secret. But before the croissant crumbs left the table, paths unfurled that would change the marrow of every last one of them.

Omar's words drifted between them like smoke from a distant fire, challenging, almost sweet in its danger. The old wall clock creaked onward, counting seconds that felt thicker than glass. Nova replayed his offer, the trouble and the spark of chance in each unguarded beat. She felt the brittle edge of betrayal ragged against her skin, yet another possibility, faint but bright, glowed through the cracks. Beneath the low, humming Paris sky, she understood. This suggestion was the doorway, not the door, and through it she might finally thread herself free of the fraying net that had first caught her weeks ago.

Nights and corners of scattered papers had stacked into this instant. Every alley she had weighed, every silence she had weighed, now interwove like starlines on a planner. Nova straightened her spine, fingers steady. She scripted the cypher, each stroke a whisper running rivers beyond rivers. Lagos woke hours later. Kofi's sleep-muzzed eyes scanned the screen, the single column of sigils, and his frown darkened into certainty. Beneath its lacquered face, the message uncoiled like a long-kept secret. In the meantime, Elena's search scented the same thread. The Argentinian dusk dialled her closer toward a name half-swallowed in the dark. A hush of rusted voices outlined a figure without a face—promising, and dangerous—who might finally thread the last needle of truth through her.

Under the neon-spangled skyline of Singapore, two masked figures slipped into a dim alley, their hushed exchange the spark for a partnership no one had foreseen. Nova, through her cool, careful play, had pushed both to the same table, ready for the embers of vengeance to catch flight. The final cards were laid bare, the exile who chose darkness now baited into her own game. Excitement curled through the room like smoke, a mixture of thrill and dread that gripped the allies now pulled into the web.

Sitting slightly apart, Nova drove on—justice was the only crown that mattered. Threat upon threat mounted like storm clouds, yet her grip on the mission never wavered. With that first whispered signal, the fabric of the scheme tightened, now woven at the centre of the City that never sleeps. Paris, already trembling, would feel the tremor first, and every choice that followed would stamp the story with scars and scars of victory. The chase had truly begun.

Chapter Two

The Ghost in the Machine

The room hummed softly, sickly fluorescent lights off, greenish screen glow the only witness. Nova bent toward her setup, hands dancing the way fighters use feet—fast, fierce, certain. Briars of code scrolled vertically and horizontally, the commands obeyed as if they owed her a code of honour. Inside her mind, a quieter storm whipped loops of possible futures against a steady rock. Here, beneath the perfume of solder and old chips, she felt the world click into focus. The knot she clawed at today was clever past clever—algebra folded into Rube Goldberg. Each shard of its design slid into the following, like language and melody. Most would have shut the door, complaining of time, but Nova grinned, the private smile she offered only herself; a comet's tail of possibility bright behind her. Winding her wrist, she set a backdoor that rippled transparency across the monitor. No lights flashed, no trumpets sounded, but the little doll-like figures of her code blinked green—safe birds abandoning a birch at the first clap of thunder. She straightened, the tiny glow under her collar going calm.

In the hush of the room, every movement Nova made broke the stillness like the tolling of a bell, sending ripples that promised to travel far past the four walls she occupied. An electric sense of urgency filled the space, and she would not let her gaze leave the monitor. She understood how much hung in the balance; one misstep and the fragile chance would slip from her fingers. Time itself felt reconfigured: every tick was both a long stretch of heated forever and the sharp blink of a pupil. The sense of duty rested on her like a drenched old coat; she carried it pleased and determined because her aim was worth the weight. The letters and numbers glimmering on the screen shifted like stars in a still night sky, and a deep instinct uncoiled inside her, nudging her toward the graceful crack she had long roamed the darkness to find. In that heartbeat, she sensed the digital air bend in her favour, and a brief fire of achievement flared in her chest, a hush of triumph swept through the storm of her labour.

Then, unexpectedly, the lead fluttered away like smoke, leaving only the empty chill of unreleased possibility, and Nova felt it threatened to swallow her whole. But surrender had never seen her face; instead, the space brewed fresh fire in her chest and hardened her resolve to beat the digital monster breathing on their backs. When dawn's first light bled the sky with soft rose and fierce gold, she stood anchored in her chair, a lighthouse of restlessness, every nerve tuned to the impossible question that had already stolen weeks of sleep. The road still stretched endlessly ahead, but with every relentless keystroke, she leaned a fraction farther into the starless black, chasing the glimmer coaxing her from the edge.

The phone's insistence shattered the flat's stillness, the sound ringing on a frequency that drove into Omar's skull like a hammer. He jerked awake, fingers fumbling the receiver, the weight of sleep still smudging his eyes. 'Mmm?' his voice wobbled, sticky with night. On the line, Nova's voice was a thin wire of alarm that sliced through the fog. She reported the fragment she had yanked from the dark web—a thread thin yet vibrating, warning of a splice he and she had already chased. The pulse in his throat quickened; he quieted the abrupt revolt of his body and sat bolt upright, the night still clinging to his skin like a bad catch.

A flicker of caution nudged at Omar's mind, edging in beside the fierce urgency in Nova's voice. Was he really ready to step further into this maze of danger and lies? The stakes kept climbing, the countdown louder. He paused and inhaled, feeling the moment tilt toward a choice that could redraw his entire life. Responsibility packed the backpack he'd carried for so long, feeling heavier now. The flash of a narrow escape shot through his memory, a leftover burst of fear and doubt. He wasn't only scared for his own skin; the web of treachery they were peeling apart was already trying to lap over the whole crew. Doubt's fingers coiled tighter, making him want to pull back. Yet, the brightness of the truth sparkled too intensely to ignore, even knowing the edge of the pit was only a step away.

Omar pushed away the voice that warned him to sleep. Instead, he kept chasing the riddle that had latched onto the whole team. Piece by stubborn piece, the night kept stretching, the pattern refusing to show itself. Finally, in the quiet of a midnight hour he'd long since claimed as a second skin, he dug into a forgotten database. He found the spark—a single line of code, buried, flickering, waiting.

The shock of it slammed into him like icy wind. He felt his heart thump louder and louder—every second a countdown he could not ignore. Leaning closer to the screen, he slowed his breathing, letting the numbers slide past his eyes again. Then he caught the drift—the same tell-tale spike in too many places, connected like a chain pulling tight. The truth behind it hummed a darker note than he had ever heard. The scenarios stacked in his head, each one darker than the one before, until a single thought broke the rush and lit the room. The one link he had missed blinked like a signal flare, and suddenly the whole grid drew into fierce focus. He tasted the weight of the revelation: this was no isolated crack—this was a failing dam, and it stretched across the world. Omar pushed the screen shut with a hard clap. He would not waste the breath to wonder if the plan would survive the telling. He had to warn the others and show them the path. He felt the chill of the road ahead: half-truth, half-shadow, allies already torn by hidden agendas. Yet, the team was already moving, and he would lead them through the dark, even if the dark was the only guide they had.

The more they pried, the more they would confront forces that shattered the limits of chance, forces that twisted the actual design of the conspiracy itself, shaking the bedrock of everything they had believed.

Late night folded over the city like a closing book. Kofi, a ghost from the intelligence underworld, slipped back into a light he had sworn never to cross again. Years of cloaking his old name in smoke and false passports had given him the peace of a stranger, yet tonight that peace turned to stone. He had to warn Nova and the others before the silence of the coming storm turned to screams.

His shoes marked the wet pavement in flat whispers that carried too far. He counted every bead of the cold, every silent tread he had swallowed, until the meet's brick corners finally glowed in the night. The secret he carried pressed like a loaded pistol against his ribs. He had pulled on the last loose thread of half-forgotten rumours, and it had yanked him back into the nightmare of his old life. The thread tied the dust-storm of recent disasters to a black project he had engineered from the shadows, a ghost that still stirred in the corners of his dreams.

In a quiet alley where the city's pulse thinned to a hush, Kofi stepped into the dim glow where Nova and her crew were waiting. Burn scars and old bruises traced his skin like a map of his lost years, and his stare felt heavier than spoken warnings. When he started to talk, the weight of his caution pressed on their chests like iron. He handed them a single shard of information, and it locked into their half-formed dread with a click they all felt. The message dripped with the taste of treachery. It brought the face of their enemy into the light, the enemy who masqueraded behind polite smiles.

Kofi's voice was a ragged thread pulled straight from the fire, stitching together the lies they had learned to ignore. The real enemy was a ghost, a strategist who had spun their every move into a noose of quiet control. He named the dates and the missing faces, and the gloom rose like smoke around them. Yet even with the spectre of ruin circling, Kofi's eyes burned with a wild, stubborn ember. He might have lost every battle, but he refused to lose the last fight—he refused to bury the truth without a howl.

Kofi's warning wasn't just a story to scare them; it was a drumbeat for courage, a shout to stand and fight the dark wave rolling toward them. Under the starlit sky, Nova and her squad felt the chill of danger ahead, but the warmth of their shared courage kept the chill at bay. Together, they tightened grips on their weapons and met the brewing storm with set jaws and steady hearts.

The next morning, Elena stepped into the busy City square, the gathering already electric with murmurs and flashes. Cameras blinked like fireflies, and reporters jostled for the best angle, eyes glued to her. Taking a slow, steady breath, Elena felt the weight of the moment settle on her shoulders. The air shivered with urgency, the kind that tells you every second counts. This was no routine puzzle; the country's very future might tip on the choices she'd make here and now.   When she leaned into the microphone, silence wrapped around the crowd like night. Her voice cut through the stillness: steady, clear, the kind that owners of crowded rooms listen for. She walked everyone through the footsteps that had brought her to this square: the cold killing of a top leader; the vanishing file that everyone swore existed; and the pungent labyrinth of lies that now entwined the highest offices. Faces tightened and eyes brightened; they leaned so far forward, it was like the whole square had suddenly become one eager single breath.   Then came the moment that rippled far wider than the stone square. Elena, steady-handed and fearless, pulled forth a thick stack of pages—photocopies, scans, ink still slightly damp. She flipped one, then another, and the muttering thundered—an address, a signature, a cover-up so bold it could make the vault of silence around the palace collapse instantly. The reporters were on their feet, notebooks forgotten, cameras snapping like they were fangs in a feeding frenzy.

She hadn't slept for weeks, night after night planting one pixel after another until the ugly truth stood mocking before her: a conspiracy bent on shaking the whole region apart. The moment the evidence spread, silence gave way to gasps, which roared into panic.   The chaos didn't rattle her. Calm as a mountain, Elena laid out every careful strand of wire she had pulled: the trembling street kids, the generals who talked too much in corridors, the encrypted notes that had melted into the stone walls of a prison. Lies and half-lies had tried to drown her, yet she had swum through every current. Her resolve glimmered like a freshly-polished knife as she painted the operation that now roared in front of them. Yes, danger waited in every shadow, yet danger had never been a deal-breaker. Truth, she promised, was the only prize that mattered.   When the sun tipped low and turned the square into fire, her final word was a vow heavy as iron. She would hunt the architects to the ends of every map, to the darkest corners that fancy themselves safe. With the fire in her gaze, she stepped away from the platform, heartbeat matching the war drum, and knew the first shot of the whole game had finally cracked the air.

It was a seemingly innocuous piece of data, a single line of code buried deep within the labyrinth of the internet. But to Nova, it was the first clue in a puzzle that could unravel a conspiracy of global proportions. The internet was a maze where every door swung on a riddle and every riddle could lead the innocent to a cliff. Nova stepped into it, aware that each click could shred her.

Nova had spent too many nights crouched by a glow of a screen, hunting for one spark of data that might crack the case wide open. The work gnawed at her, but the fire of hard-won purpose kept her going. She wanted answers, and that wish never wavered. As she slid deeper into the dark web of circuits and firewalls, her virtual body felt as real as the one she'd left behind. She ghosted between spinning nodes and black lakes of lost answers, every hazard and detour a warning she'd learned to tune out. Days signed their fading names across the calendar, and the one piece she needed kept slipping away—until a barely-there pulse of data tugged her focus. It appeared like a candle flickering in a storm: a single, sideways glimmer of code curled up in a flood of numbers. At first, it could have passed for an error, a typo, or nothing at all. However, Nova felt a ticking lock and leaned in closer. With a surgeon's touch, she pulled apart every angle, every digit, searching for the whisper that might one day grow into a thousand words of truth.

The mind-blowing moment hit when she peeled back layers of code and saw the hidden glyph flash a time and place: a hush-hush summit walled in concrete in the centre of Brussels. Her blood surged like a tide, and every watchful neuron lit up—the lightning bolt she'd chased through sleepless weeks. No second thoughts flickered. Nova dispatched the code straight to her team of shadows—analysts, hackers, linguists, and a roller-skating forensics whiz, all spinning in separate day and night cycles, each with their unique skills and expertise. Every word and emoji crawled through quantum locks and triple-layer dark webs until her squad glittered to life on mirror walls. Distributed and yet forged, they sealed a fireproof oath: rip the mask off the rot hiding beneath everyday calm. Clue primed, the hive spun into motion. Holograms painted the Brussels skyline, rail and runway links glowing like a nervous pulse. Cells chirruped, drones blue-printed in Berlin garages. From São Paulo to a dust-hazed rooftop in Delhi, code crawled into the arteries of protocol. The team, a constellation of vivid dots, aimed at a single blink of time. The plan hummed: they'd slip into the square, pocket the thread, and yank hard. The moment fastened into the future—tiny, dangerous, but already shimmering with promise.

For Nova and her crew, the weeks ahead could tip into either victory or letdown, yet they chose to move boldly into the danger in the name of justice.

Through the shimmering veil of the digital realm, Nova charted hidden corridors and wove together her squad. Each recruit was chosen not for raw talent alone, but for the steady fire of purpose in their chests. Omar, the quiet genius of codes, carried the weight of ghosts yet signed on the moment he realised the danger was real, and that solving it meant more than ego. Elena, tough as wire, was a reporter willing to chase the story into the teeth of fire. Kofi, a ghost from the intelligence underworld, tipped them off about the traps that lay beneath the blacked-out maps. United, they blossomed into a silent, global unit, pulled together by one beating heart: to rip the mask off the threat creeping their way. Miles of ocean and city between them became a single, glowing table of shared sights and whispered plans.

Through shimmering holograms and channels locked tighter than a safe, they dug into bits of data dragged up from the digital dark. Every meet felt like a secret mission where each voice carried a spark: the coder who spoke in algorithms, the ex-field agent who slid tactical maps into view, the junior analyst whose instincts caught the slipstream. Pressure squeezed them, a vice of ticking clocks and hidden watchers, but under the pressure, a quiet heat fused them, a shared spark hotter than secret motives.

Arguments flared like errant sparks. Old grudges, unvoiced for months, leapt into the daylight. Angles of attack widened, some eyeing the prize, others guarding personal losses, and the web they'd woven strained where they'd thought it strongest. Messages that used to dash clear now snare in loops of who-meant-what. Nova stood in the dark circle of each new meeting, heartbeat steadying the shaky cams, knowing that to lose the knot now was to lose everything, the city and each still-whole part of the city.

Her strong will and fearless energy steadied the team while they tried to pull together the scattered dreams and spark the last glow of togetherness. Even though the cracks among them were widening, their shared will stay as solid as steel. Inside their chat rooms, the sound of courage rose like music while they faced the dark clouds piling up ahead. A storm of doubt and anger began to quiet, replaced by a fresh drive that wove them into an even tighter thread. Piece by piece, they built their plan, the once-scattered fragments sliding into a single, dread-sharp pattern that sent tremors through every pixel of their shared world.

The virtual conference room buzzed with heat as muted faces stared back from the grid of tiles. Nova, the shadowy leader no one had ever really met, marked the tight line of Omar's jaw and the dry fire in Elena's gaze. They were spinning deeper into the labyrinth of codes, and the night's task no longer felt like a mission—now it felt like a sentence. Omar, genius turned wild card, shouted for a strike that could burn their cover to cinders. Kofi, the abacus mind of the crew, measured each move like a guard at a chessboard, and the split grew wider with every keystroke. Elena lived for puzzles, yet every fragment she turned sewed more doubt. Loyalty to the crew warred with the pull of the truth they had chased through smoke and blood. She'd stared down guns that had no opinion of her, yet tonight the real weight dug into her. The others could mask their faces, but the mask of secrecy was cracking. Sleep would not come until the last piece fell.

Inside the flickering silences of their shared channels, trouble gnawed beneath the polished surface of their brotherhood. Each of them carried ghosts—grudges, broken oaths, secrets sharpened by loss—little shards that cut every time they brushed too close. Past betrayals loomed above their common mission like storm clouds, ready to spill. Nova, ever the vigilant shadow, saw the first misquoted joke explode into blaring accusations. She drew a slow, steady breath and stepped between the sparks, unfurling a quiet authority that felt almost like a hand reaching across the gulf. Gravity and kindness threaded through her voice, turning thunder into thunderhead. "We're the only side we've got," she said, and the line held just long enough for the storm to hesitate. When the last distant echo of anger faded, the Quiet gathered breath again, more whole than it had been a moment before. Cohesion was a wobbly seed starting to crack, still too raw to forget the heat that had just passed through it. Dissent still slid beneath their skin like aftershocks, but for the moment, the space between them had cooled to the colour of trust.

Forged in the fire of every setback, the group finally forged their bonds, ready to step into the darkness together, their hearts driven by one mission and the ironclad will to face whatever eavesdropper was responsible for the incoming storm.

For a week, the squad had sparked like downed power lines, every argument louder than the next. Omar the silent gear head and Nova the cyber-shadow could not bridge the gulf between the map and the screen. The clock was a hammer on the anvil of their guts, arguing faster than they could think. Then, when everything was losing colour, a single glint cut the grey. An old intercept had surfaced—scattered code that whispered of cloaked figures gathering in the bowels of Vienna. Their first real sword in the fight. The fragments fell into place like sharded glass, and for a heartbeat, caution cracked into something brighter. Omar calibrated the old triangulator, and the flickering cursor circled a ghost line—rows of vanished corridors only old ghosts and street legends knew. Nova keyed up layers of the city, threads of alibi and shadow, and sketched a braid that would let them watch without the watchers ever hearing a footfall. Together they nudged the spark into flame, ready for the next beat of the machine.

The stakes were as high as the cathedral spires slicing the twilight, and quitting was off the table. The team stepped into the stain-dark subway tunnels of Vienna with the quiet snap of long-rehearsed timing. Bodies moved in a flashing blend of armour and shadow, each person locked into their part of the greater clockwork. The hush down here was a bone-deep cold; the hush was the mission numb and alive. Each boot-fall rang hollow, a ghost of a stir, a promise of the fight yet to come. Night and then night again folded into itself. The heaviness in the passage was the weight of the grey-sky pause before a lightning crack. A scatter of voices finally spilt through the vent slits, thin as a spider thread, the quiet cue the team had held their breath for.

Tiny drones ticked out of backpacks, night eyes searching for the meeting's hidden fire. A bundle of digital equipment unfolded, each screen a thin window into the underground smoke. Palms slick with a cold panic, the operatives pressed the controls, decoding a flood of mask-shaded chatter and ghostly tokens. The snared streams twisted and knotted, but then a shape began to lift out of the static: a glowing river of handshakes, fake passports, and submachine-part buys, all rerouted to the same spreading hand. Each red dot pulled tighter, all the stray pieces seeming to obey a single distant pulse. After too long in the electronic desert, one name arrived on the scrolling tide: a money-shifting ghost with spire-width fingers and offices on every continent's ragged edge.

The news hit the team like a thunderclap, shoving any last shred of doubt straight out the window. One single, crackling feed had shown them a shadowy web that stretched farther than any of them had dared imagine. In that flicker, they had seen the gears grinding toward a crisis that could rattle the whole planet. Suddenly, the path ahead was ablaze with cold certainty: they had dropped deeper into the night than they'd planned, and the darkness was now alive beneath their feet. That same darkness now glittered before them, a lure and a trap, daring them to keep going, daring them to misstep. Every tick of the clock was a crack of a starting pistol, counting off the tiny units of time before their enemies struck back. That ticking was in their bones, in their ears, pressuring them—and the knowledge they'd just YANKED into the light pressed back harder, a vice on their ribs.

The clock's red numbers blinked in the dark like the eyes of some bored giant waiting to forget them. They crowded around the table, faces tight as a violin string, and the clock counted them down, tick tick tick, like the voice of a judge. Nova's hands danced over the keys, chasing data through the open oceans of the web, fingers moving with a speed that came from stubbornness, not caffeine. Omar darted his gaze from window to window, tracing lines of code and conflict, trying to grab the half-formed conclusions that sparkled just out of reach.

The electricity of the moment pressed down on them like a thick cloud. The First Lead had struck a match in each heart, pushing them forward with a burning certainty that mocked the impossible. Kofi's clear voice sliced through the steady buzz, each word a hammer against the stakes. "We're out of time," he said, resolve iron at the core. "One more minute and we cross the line we can't uncross." Elena lifted her eyes, scanning every friend, her steady courage a lit lantern. "We can't let this thread slip now," she said, her voice steady as stone. "We are the hands that will finally pull the answer free." The weight of shattering truth settled deep inside, lighting a wildfire of shared will. Together, they laboured, fingers flying over keys and charts, their bond a chain stronger than steel, forged in the same hunger for the truth. The clock's metronome marched on, each tick ringing in their ears like a drum of either hope or disaster.

Every ticking second drew the puzzle apart, offering sparkling hints of the hidden truth that danced just un-reachable. Side by side, they pressed on, stretching their know-how and their willpower, refusing to let time fence them in. The clock ticking down toward discovery had start-ed, and their never-give-up spark shone like a lighthouse, lighting the winding, shadowy corridors of doubt.

Chapter Three

The Brussels Connection

The team gathered in a basement room lit only by flickering bulbs, every brain working together to trace the twisting threads of secrets now gathering in Brussels. This was the critical hour, the one that called for both caution and a clear vision. They leaned closer to the map spread on the table, the ink still shiny where the latest tip had landed. They needed someone who could disappear into the city and come back with answers—someone who not only understood every back alley and crooked stairway, but also carried a handful of trusted informers in every neighbourhood. Someone trusted. Kofi's name broke the silence, cutting through the dimness like a signal beam. He could slip into the city's living skin and tell them where the pulse was fastest. He lived the story now unfolding, which turned him into the one person who could guide them through the night. They weighed the risks of drawing him in, of pushing him deeper into the fire, and the balance tipped solidly in favour of the move. Kofi would be the key that turned the lock on Brussels's darkest corners, opening doors and dark corners that remained shut to outsiders. They dimmed the bulbs, huddled close, and pushed the decision already stamped in silence into words: within hours, Kofi would be on the move, and the city would begin to surrender its secrets to them through him.

Each member of the unit recognised the peril of bringing a civilian into their covert mission. Yet, the cold clock of their countdown had no mercy for caution. They steeled their nerves, and the road that opened before them shimmered with mysteries and risks, with Kofi now the bright point around which their daring scheme spun.

Kofi confronted a fork in the road that could redraw the boundaries of his life. For years, he had worn the badge of devotion to the Service like a second skin, honouring every summons with pride. Still, the faces of his family nested in the back of his mind, a quiet insurgent that whispered of dinners missed and birthdays unmarked. Their memory warmed him, but also twisted the knife of doubt. He longed for the easy blend of laughter and argument that filled his old flat—the smell of fried plantain and the jokes that never grew stale. Duty, however, pressed him onward, its voice steady as a metronome, trading portion after portion of his life for secrets to keep the world unbroken.

Sweet faces danced across Kofi's mind like autumn leaves caught in a gust, each one igniting a dozen different feelings all at once. He heard his kids' bright, ringing laughter, felt his partner's familiar, calming arms, and caught that everyday scent of home that both comforted and haunted him. Those little pieces of his past murmured softly, begging him to listen. But duty loomed like a storm tower, its cold, steady clang locking him to a place he could not leave. He wondered if it was fair to place his own aching heart beneath that of a mission bigger than himself. Were the risks so grave that he could not, for once, choose the life he longed for? Torn by the pull of love and the pull of honour, Kofi stood in a dark crossroads of his own making. A thick mist of doubt hid the neat lines of right and wrong, turning every possible path into a shadow shape he could not measure. Each road carried its own heavy cost, each one wrapping his heart in a braid of choices he could not unweave. To turn his back on the mission would feel like cutting the thread of his own name, like spitting on the vow he had made on the first day he fastened the uniform, the weight of which had long ago merged with the shape of his bones.

If he ignored the quiet tug of family, he risked losing the delicate ties that kept him human. The idea of drifting alone in regret chilled him. The gulf between duty and blood now faded into something he couldn't label, a slippery mix of love and sacrifice. How could he cross that landscape, where each footfall bore the weight of lives resting on his steadiness? Inside the storm of his heart, Kofi lingered on the razor edge of a choice that would carve the future for him and for the watchers, who counted on one single guardian prowling the twilight.

Amid Kofi's pull between duty and love, a hidden circle of power brokers plotted a chilling, glittering snare. They moved with quiet, blade-smooth exactness, laying the quaking groundwork for a lie so dense it would rewrite what people dared call truth. Kofi's private storm, he would discover, was about to dissolve into a darker, more expansive ocean of covert statecraft.

A small group of shadowy planners carried out this false flag with icy focus, pulling clever strings so the whole world would see what they wanted it to see—and nothing more. One by one, they triggered a chain of events meant to bend public opinion while secret moves continued deep in Brussels. No twist was left to chance; every weapon of misdirection was polished to hide their relentless ambition. Masks were polished, names were borrowed, and a hidden world fused with the everyday one. An interrupted dance at a train platform became a code, a file folder left in a café held a talisman, and plain greetings became whispers of a grand design. Underneath the harmless, every flick of the wrist, every dropped pencil, was a carefully calculated stitch sewing the illusion into everyday sight. Newsrooms swallowed the fabricated tale whole; it slipped into every headline and every news alert, pumping its venom into the public mind. Ordinary people, in the wrong place at the wrong moment, were moved like chess pieces; their thoughts choreographed, their feelings choreographed by the shimmering illusion that radiated all around them. The false flag grew into a thick fog, veiling the true architects, binding the crowd in a cage of synthetic truths.

While most people went about their daily lives, a hidden concert of lies swelled to deafening volume, weaving itself into every conversation we have. The story, carefully invented, found a home in every government office, sounding practised and serious enough to mask the betrayal underneath. Cloaked in the colours of truth, this artful deception was about to decide the future of entire countries, its makers hidden from view, free from any sense of right or wrong.

Kofi faced the company's number 2 man, the bench-press-surveyor belt buckle bright in the half-dark. Kofi's coffee-cold eyes measured every tick subsurface, looking for the blue shimmer of caution in the executive's irises. Shadows trailing every square inch of the small room carried the ghosts of every interview Kofi had ever lost, and Kofi inched that risk for the last time. His notebook remained closed, the cover faintly trembling with the future he had first smelled rats and plasma months back.

The executive, maned and scent-marked in armour-guarded confidence, parried the standard questions with rehearsed warmth and a smile that could open a vault. Kofi didn't go for the vault, didn't telegraph tic, didn't blink. Ten years of notebook-dark instincts sealed the fissile rods of the interview, every inquiry shrinking back, missile-like, to the single centrifuge he was afraid to name. Memory-bullets from the 2021 offshore lodgement and the 2022 bottle-ship recall sliced through the sports gloss of his gracious opponent's smile, first a wobble in the boot-heel, then a little nicotine-ash twitch in the corner of a jaw that had never trembled.

Before the executive felt the term mouth-burned in his throat, Kofi had finished painting the question's skeleton in his head: was it really easier to swamp a risk column with recycled stock than to fly cargo into cabin-press blue? The room had 72 microphones, and the ceiling had a hurry-up cough that tested Kofi's link-discipline. With every soft repeat and every half-seed Kofi dropped, he kept his own name out of the carcass, kept his own ego out of the jury box. One more question was coming.

Kofi chased the story like a hound on the scent, driven by a sense of duty that burned hotter than a summer pavement. He knew the facts he hunted could send ripples across the continent. Slowly, he watched the prominent executive's mask begin to crack, a bead of sweat tracing a crooked line down a marble forehead. The room felt different then, as if a scale had tipped in favour of the small man with the quiet voice. When the flood came, the executive's calm smile broke into a jagged grin of defeat. Kofi, calm as a hand opening a pistachio, seized the moment and steered the talk to the rotting core of the cover-up. He pressed for the names, the dates, the money trails that danced just unreachable. He knew the truth was a shy deer that would bolt at the slightest hush; you had to move slow, aim steady, and never quit. Piece by piece, he dropped the shy mask of the ordinary reporter and let the blade of the investigator shine through. His questions whispered, but the weight behind them burned like the desert sun. Kofi played the long game, and the truth, however slippery, would one day flop gasping at his feet.
In the hush of that shadowy room, where voice and feeling seemed to breathe the same air, Kofi kept at the brittle truth the way a keeper of the flame guards the last fire on a long night. His work showed that a steady mind and a steady heart combine to pry the tangled, hidden things apart.

Kofi had always trusted that his fingers could slide beneath on-ramp after on-ramp of digital locks, yet this time the leak of the leak slid away from him like quicksilver. The clock was a visitor that grew restless with every heartbeat, and Kofi felt the world's urge behind him. The screen's cold light caught the sweat on his brow; the runes on the pane flickered and re-formed like a dream half-remembered. Kofi leaned closer, lips muted in prayer, waiting for a blur of sense to break the swirl. Every tap of a key was pressed with the weight of the coming moment, stacking the silent pieces of the dark message one on top of the next. The twist of symbols spoke of a foe smarter than he had pictured at first—a shadow long enough to reach around the horizon. Days drifted into days, and still Kofi pressed on, the flame of his will refusing to bow.

He dived deep into the neon circuits of the network, sliding between layers of smoke and misdirection. The code flickered mockingly, twisting just out of reach, testing his brain and his grit. Yet Kofi never bowed to provocation; every new block only steeled his will. Amid the hush of blinking servers and the muted hum of the data centre, a quiet spark of clarity lit up his monitor. Tucked inside the twisted splay of letters and looped logic, he spotted a faint, crooked line—one that refused the disciplined hush of proper encryption. That crooked line glittered like an unguarded door. When its meaning crystallised, Kofi felt blood thunder in his ears. The line was not just a broken rule; it was the nerve of a plotted storm that could warp borders and ignite headlines. He inhaled, summoned every nerve cell, and began to pull the crooked thread. As it unwound, layer after layer of dark meaning fell away, revealing a scheme better left buried in the dark.

What crawled up from the heart of the code crushed even Kofi's wildest nightmares: an elegant map for collapse, drawn by faceless players armed with resources the world never counted and intentions darker still. When he finally read it, the chill of absolution and dread wound tight around his ribs. Cracking the puzzle had never been the prize; the prize was what it had unlocked—entry to a game he had never agreed to play. Night fell sharper now, the towers of Brussels like black teeth on the skyline, and Kofi sensed not victory but the soft opening of a door into a silent, raging conflict—every second now a decision that could edit tomorrow's history.

Kofi's footsteps in Brussels were engineered, not borrowed; the city pulled him like a magnet, pushing him deeper into corridors only private nightmares dare name. Grey stone and glimmering glass blurred into a single pulse of expectation. With every alley he crossed, the responsibility clung tighter, a literal weight like a belt of bricks. The city breathed somewhere under the skin of the day, breathing stories of whispering rooms and agendas that never spoke daylight.

Moving through the busy streets, Kofi felt the city's calm surface crack open, letting him see the tiny signs and whispers lying just beneath the ordinary scene. Every face passing him felt heavier, each one possibly carrying the thread he needed or the edge of a trap. Here, truth and shadow traded places so easily that caution became the only way to stay alive. He followed a message that read like smoke, pushing himself through the veins of Brussels. At the same time, the great grey buildings of the European quarter loomed above like stone giants guarding secrets. With every step, he balanced on the thin edge of lying and finding out, knowing that one wrong turn could make everything collapse. He could not afford to miss a single clue. The burden of the truth pressed down like a stone in his chest. When darkness spilt across the city, Kofi's path brought him to a hidden meeting soaked in silence and danger. He moved through narrow streets where the light was thin and met people whose faces told nothing, their voices sliding by like rain on glass. Their sentences danced around the real meaning, and he felt a hidden web vibrating just under the stone. This web reached not just into alley corners but into the very rooms where the city's future was decided.

Inside this tangle of lies, Kofi felt himself sliding headfirst into a game where every glance might be a knife and every handshake a contract with the devil. The shiny skin of the city glittered above. At the same time, the sewers of power and deception hummed below, each flush of a toilet a reminder that someone, somewhere, was flushing the evidence away. Kofi pressed on, each alley narrower and each neon flicker more judgmental, the map in his pocket reshaping itself with every half-heard rumour and retracted breath. Faces in doorways offered half-truths; the other halves were already sold to the highest bidder. Step by step, Kofi felt the truth turning in his hand like an heirloom dagger—beautiful, sharp, and needed—but it could also cut his throat if the wrong hand grabbed it.

The room felt like a forgotten locker. The single bulb hung like a dying star, barely denting the shadows. Kofi sat opposite the CEO, mask flat and eyes wide open, a fisherman waiting for the river to boil. The man's skin was a map of past storms and silent lands, and when he opened his mouth, the words poured out like old, rusted coins—clinking with guilt no mint would ever touch. The man's voice shook, a tremor that travelled from his throat to the ether, each syllable a confession laid out on a table no one wanted to see. With a shuddering breath, he stepped onto a path of remembrance, dragging Kofi into a tour of dark moments that had rerouted rivers of history. Piece by piece, the ex-CEO stitched together a garment of betrayals, stolen powers, and secrets sewn under the table. Every sentence made Kofi's skin prick. The old man's sober pieces of truth flickered, charts of the hidden world inside the inside world. Kofi saw, with growing dread, that clocks were ticking faster than anyone had guessed. The CEO's voice quaked as he confessed to shadow missions crossing oceans, missions that had, one by one, loosened the bolts of global safety. Each new piece unwound another corner of the puzzle, dragging Kofi down into corridors darker than he'd dreamed. The burden of the secrets settled like lead in his chest. He knew—he knew—that every move he dared to make from that thin, slicing second would swing wide the fate-doors of millions. The tale slipped into silence, the last word a smoke-tinged threat that wound itself around Kofi, whispering that powers far grander than his own were, right now, watching and waiting.

Stepping out of the office, the CEO's final statement bounced around in his head like an alarm siren, laying out the first move in a fight that would shape the destiny of every person alive.

Kofi's heart raced as he replayed the CEO's last words in his mind, the conference room's smoky edges closing around him. For the first time, the normally patient analyst felt the cold knife of fear. Business, he'd learned, was often a slalom through greed and half-truths, but this felt like the first mile of a blacked-out ravine. Somewhere inside the murmured cables and sterile servers, facts smaller than a comma had been arranged to masquerade as generosity. Kofi leaned closer to the glowing screen, fingers moving like a lock-picking pianist. The data slides had masked a low-frequency hum: a signal so carefully tuned that default filters missed it. When Kofi separated out the chorus of sales graphs and customer records, he heard it whispering over and over, a ghost slipping concealed minutes into the night. The room dropped a few degrees, and so did Kofi. Night after night, he replayed code and countercode, his only company the soft thud of energy drinks and the bitter taste of his own quickened breath. The signal had no sender and no register, yet it carried lines that ought to have lived only in con-ference-password vaults. Piece by piece, the puzzle moved from annoyance to confession: some second spine of the company had learned to forget the light. Kofi felt the cold breath of the unknown on his neck and smiled anyway. If he had to pull the secret out drop by drop, he would.

Every line of code Kofi peeled back felt like another brick pressed against his ribs. The signal inside it was a twisted arrow, scratching out directions to a scheme that could frac-ture their entire network and cut down everything he cared about. His fingers shook, caught between terror and the electric pull of fight, yet his will didn't waver. The burden of the truth pressed like a black cloud, swallowing the comfort of the room he'd known for years. Each tap on the keyboard rang out louder than the last, a countdown that dragged him closer to an enemy still draped in shadow. The truth was unfolding, yet Kofi knew the signal was only a chink in the surface, a warning of a bigger, darker surge ready to swallow him whole. Alone in the flicker of the monitors, he promised himself he would chase the truth to the very last breath. The signal flickered like a hidden pulse, daring him to step into a whirlwind that swelled bigger and louder than anything he'd ever dared to imagine.

The hidden signal finally showed its fangs and froze Kofi at his desk. That harmless 3D barcode burned into the back of the CEO's business card was never just a logo; it was a doorway into a network that dwelled beneath the polished surface of corporate life. Kofi watched the seconds tick and felt the weight of what was coming. The beacon had drifted awake, and its glow now promised a storm that could sweep Brussels—and the entire continent—off its feet.

Digging deeper, Kofi discovered this was not a one-off

glitch but a cold, chess-like escalade meant to shatter every political and economic pillar. The floor felt unsteady beneath his training shoes as he tracked the broth of signal, safe house, and safe deposit box. Each candle flame of the network burned a carefully choreographed role—intel drips, viral fractures of truth, market nudges. The scheme was uglier, slippier, and more complex than anything Kofi's counter-ops unit had ever cracked.

Now, with the clock ticking like a heart ready to burst, Kofi stood at the dizzying crossroad of loyalty and love. The UN's duty badge weighed like lead on one shoulder; his wife's and daughter's laughter rang like a beacon on the other. The choice clawed at his gut.

The line between staying safe and staying on the job vanished the minute Kofi realised, each decision he made now carried the force of a hammer against the fate of the innocent trapped in the blast radius. The warning light flickered like a heartbeat, and he pulled together a mismatched band of survivors, each one marked in a way the light won't ever catch. They stepped into the twisted alleys of Brussels, the city itself lying like a secret in a bleeding wound, and with every new door they forced, the darkness folded back to show one more layer of lies. Kofi felt the rise and the weight of it; one bad signal, one wrong word, and the odds of rescue could turn into the odds of a funeral. Pressure clamped around his lungs, but he calculated anyway. Out here, the game was smoke, mirrors, and secrets guarded by guns; gradually, a clearer picture began to surface. The picture was a lie he'd once sworn to protect. The stillness before the first wave of ruin was almost deafening; he felt every heartbeat like a countdown. Kofi promised the night he'd meet the killer at the door, even if the price was everything he loved still breathing.

The signal had blown open a storm of doubt, and the silent calling of truth flickered in the black, daring Kofi to wander into the heart of power and lies.

In the hush of the Brussels office, the lights were low, and the air tasted of wire and worry. Kofi leaned forward, spine straight, and let the new signal burn a fresh line beneath the ruined skyline. A clock had started to tick, louder than the buzz of the overhead lamp. He opened the fresh layer of code, heart and head synchronised, and let his fingers unknit the silence, pressing each key like a note in a score only he could hear. Lines of red, green, black: they peeled away from each other and then folded over, and the shape of the trap took hourglass form. He pressed harder, and the chill slipped beneath his ribs – there was no ordinary enemy here. It wore the cloak of the unseen, and every cut it made dripped pure night, leaving no numbered line on any headstone. The dark was mapped in loops and datagrams, and now the lines began to snap into geometry – a chamber of mirrors that ran further than he had dared to guess.

Kofi chased the truth like a firefly in a storm, only to find each answer turning into a new question, a new shadow to follow. Still, one truth burned brighter than the rest: he had to find the evil that hid behind the screens before the world burned. Time stretched and shrank like a taut wire, and he lived a thousand lives in one night—a blur of coding, coffee, and the growl of silence. Inside his head, the enemy never wore a face but roared in stolen data and broken firewalls, daring him to blink. Outside, cities slept, but the stakes never did. Kofi dug deeper, deeper, in a place where colours swap and masks don masks, where reason waits to be chased. Each fragment of code, each leak of static, each unfamiliar line on a map, spun him in a new orbit. Exhaustion pinched his eyelids, but the weight on his chest felt heavier than sleep. Kofi straightened his back, adjusted the collar on a shirt stained by many nights, and kept moving. Night-dark and neon-bright, the screen threw his face back at him. And in that glow, a small flame flickered: the stubborn faith that truth was a seed which, if pushed into the dirt of night, would one day break into a sun.

Chapter Four

THE RUSSIAN GAMBIT

The night had just opened its curtain when a strange black tide rolled through Moscow. Once-gleaming towers froze into cold black stone, their thousands of windows snuffed like breaths. The grid trembled, shuddered, and the city dropped into chilling silence. An electric sort of dread sparked between the corridors.

At the heart of the city, the Kremlin became a black puzzle piece against the clear night, its golden towers swallowed. Inside, hurried voices crackled then vanished. Screens grew still, lines turned mute, and the pulse of data that usually raced through government nerves turned to rusted air. The words "state of emergency" vanished before they could be shouted.

Outdoors, the night turned feral. Signals froze, and traffic spun into a furious ballet of horns and headlights that only made the night darker. Buses ground to a halt, their neon route numbers cut off like defeat. Bars and cafés went dark mid-song, leaving people standing sway-backed between missing friends and missing maps. The cityscape, usually a river of neon fists, folded into pipe-black nothing, and Moscow felt itself breathing alone and afraid.

The emergency sirens keened, slicing through the twilight, yet still the city trembled. Fire trucks, ambulances, and police cars crawled the ruined roads like slow-motion phantoms, their lights struggling against the thick, bruised night that choked every corner of Moscow. Telephone and web lines lay severed, as if a giant hand had snatched away the glow of distant screens and hollowed out the chatter of millions. The blackout had struck like a punch, and the city was still gasping. Rumours spilt onto cracked sidewalks like spilt salt, sharp and superstitious. Experts were silent on the cause, and the ordinary crowd filled the silence with unease. Was it sabotage? An unfortunate accident? Or something worse, something that gave a cruel pleasure to the darkness? Hidden in that unresolved doubt was a dread that clung to the skin. Beneath the asphalt arteries, in the damp and circulatory tunnels of the metro and ruined loops of garages, figures moved. They were dressed to vanish and watchful as the grave. The blackout had gifted them a cloak of night thick enough to hide explosives, codes, or worse, yet transparent enough that even the nervous rats skittered quieter. On encrypted lines and whispered meet-ups, they exchanged green glows and maps of decommissioned zones, counting on a Moscow too stunned to strike back. Hours folded like the collapsing blinds of a dying train, and it was obvious: the darkness was not merely the absence of streetlights. It was a living membrane that pressed against the skin of the city, waiting, designed to conceal the next stroke of the hand that meant to do harm.

The bleak truth crashed over her: Moscow was caught in a war that nothing a fuse box or a rescue crew could mend—a conflict that could drag Russia itself down a darkness no map had ever marked.

Omar's capsule was a mine of garbled chats, invisible money trails, and blink-and-miss audio that sketched a ghostly outline of the Russian play. The absurd volume of the haul, harvested by a phantom who signed only with a skull, jarred Nova like frostbite. While her fingers raced over the keys, the scatter of ones and zeroes began to rearrange, aligning into a script of invisible hands, every fingerprint leading her closer to a guarded box in the Kremlin. Every decrypted byte thudded like a heartbeat louder than her own, whispering of smoke and mirrors the leaders had already inhaled. The countdown was no longer hypothetical; it was a pulse that threatened to outpace her. With every blink, Nova sensed the globe tilting, the fulcrum of her laptop. The answer to Russia's last play lay stewing in Omar's stolen pantry, and she was the only guest. Still, as she unfurled the latest hash, a chill skated up her spine, as if the darkness had learned her name.

It was a headlong dash against an enemy that had more wealth and a colder heart than she had ever seen, and Nova could taste the danger on the back of her tongue. She pushed forward anyway, full of grit and the stubborn certainty that stopping was not a choice. The entire world's order was teetering, and surrender was the one word she could not allow to pass her lips. Inside the tangled forest of ones and zeros, a weak glint of possibility flickered at the edge of her vision, the secret that might tilt the tide back to her side. But from the dark, invisible hands were already working to make sure that Omar's fire hose of secrets opened only to a bloody price. With every letter, she hammered and every function she rewrote, the black curtain hiding the Kremlin's move grew a little thinner. The clock was peeling seconds like paint, and the heat was rising, but Nova refused to flinch. She channelled every skill she had, sliding through the red-lit corridors of cyberspace with the coolness of a surgeon. The barrier between gadgets and cloak-and-dagger had stretched out of shape. She was one painstaking move in the longest, most dangerous game of chess anyone had ever played—where a single slip could end not only her game but the game of every nation.

Deep in the maze of Omar's data gift, Nova uncovered a secret that rippled through the hidden corridors of power—plots that blurred maps and upended ideologies, built with cold precision and ruthless vision. The jagged edges of a bigger picture clicked together, and she knew this was only the first curve of a dangerous path that would push her further than she'd ever been pressed.

With a hawk's eye, Nova attacked the gift. The code

strained against her every nerve, its locks layered like a magician's show, yet her mind was a spring wound tight. She traced the curling, electric strands and, beneath noise, found hush—figures, dates, and ghost signatures that began to hum in cruel harmony. The data was a genome of betrayal, and every barcode she scanned whispered: this matters more than you dare guess; falling here means ruin.

Her deep dive into the data unearthed a hidden pit so wide and dark it threatened to swallow the world whole, and Nova felt the tick of every lost second like a warning drum. Gritting her jaw, she sorted every thread of evidence, readying a briefing for her closest allies, fully aware they were no longer facing a single rival but a hidden hand that could tighten around every government and silently choke the light out of entire cities. Nova's report felt like the first little crack in a dam, letting the river of possibility surge toward an inevitable, monumental clash—one that would carve the fate of entire nations into the unforgiving stone of tomorrow.

The briefing room hushed like a held breath when Elena slid the drive into the computer, every gesture tight and trembling with purpose. The screen blinked alive, a sickly green light tracing the angles of her jaw. Rows of code unfurled like a dark waterfall, and she, perched forward in her chair, flew her fingertips over the keyboard, motioned and silent as a pianist chasing the last perfect chord. More than data scrawled there; she felt the very breath of the world willing her hands to move. For three moons she had worked under a shrouded sky, crafting the illusion so flawless that the heart of truth itself would tremble and bend, and in a heartbeat the ship's keel would swing the other way.

Elena had memorised Kofi's gestures, matched every tilt of his head, studied his laughter, and even hunted down old rumours and forgotten blog comments to craft a copy that would fool every watcher. It proved again that she could twist the digital world into whatever shape she wanted, and now she planned to set that shape loose. When the simulation hit the last loading bar, silence tightened around the lab like a vice. Everyone could taste how dangerous the moment was. One flaw, one nerve flee, and the whole mission could collapse. Yet Elena stayed calm, her voice steady like a lighthouse signal, and she believed this one shot could swing the tide of a dozen fractured nations. At last, the display flared bright and Kofi's face filled the screen, eyes sparkling and voice firm, delivering a new speech destined to redraw borders. No professional, no spy, no seeker of truths could catch the sliver of difference. Her creation was a masterwork of code and deceit, merging what was real and what was never real into a single, chilling heartbeat. The team stayed frozen, awe and dread balanced inside them, the air heavy with the storm of what they had just done.

The risks of revealing their illusion loomed large, yet everyone at the table knew playing it close to the vest was their only shot. Truth was now a designer drug, custom-cut to soften any conscience, and their contrivance might be the distillate that reversed the high. Lose it, and nothing but cracks to the core would remain. Elena fell back in her chair, her eyes locked on the hologram of Kofi, every pore and twitch a confession. Inside her, chaos and clarity warred; still, only one principle cut through: justice would be the last outfit they let the law fit on them. The geopolitical board was about to receive a pawn masquerading as a queen, and the aftershocks would outlast the oceans that carried them. Good or ill, the fable Kofi had built on borrowed electrons was now the single keel beneath the keel of every planted truth they still dared to ship.

The chase had folded itself into the spent sleep of the Siberian forest, and Kofi could not remember the last time safety had a dialect. The cabin sat like a ghost's last thought, roof under a blanket of slate sky, walls pale as the teeth of forgotten wolves, and the only companions were the slow breathing of trees. His rank was now only a ghost's rank, yet each fibre of the new disguise itched like morning frost on exposed skin. The intelligence he had once moved like a second breath was now a blade, and betrayal had cut the lens he once trusted to show only the sky above.

Inside the small cabin, its walls still holding memories of a brighter past, Kofi looked for a moment at a world that had almost forgotten. He inventoried the few items on the warped table, counting dried roots and a scrap of meat, and accepted the truth of his life: solitude had come in its cruellest form, binding him with a rope of broken alliances and unanswered names. Neighbours had once offered bread, and raids had three fires, now the smoke rose only for him, and the only trust left was his empty hands. The flames shifted, painting the ceiling with red and grey, and in the flicker of that small warmth, Kofi allowed himself a breath. He could almost hear the rally song that had once bound the company sound in his ears; the song now rested in silence. Loyalty had been a blade he'd worn sharp; now the blade had dulled on too many unanswered faces, and he felt its weight drag down the centre of his chest. Safety had slipped from foot races on ridges to this cabin locked by bark and wind; flees of intrigue, not foot soldiers, now marked the path of his breath. Outside, a pine cracked, the wind slipped between leaves, and Kofi felt the pulse of the night swell. Each sound grew, a drumbeat in a still square, and the walls felt thinner. His old body, trained in the rhythms of living and leaning, acknowledged the drum; the sound was not the cabin talking, it was the world counting.

Still, in the silence that swallowed the wild, a spark of defiance flared inside him, lighting the determination to grasp the truth and step back into the light that fear had driven him from. Here, on the edge of the earth, hours and minutes had no weight; the wild wore the crown and the blade, shaping him into a stranger to stars and sun. Dawn folded into dusk after dusk into dawn, Kofi's feet scarring the earth as he wrestled wind and rain, the slow crawl of time, and the harder crawl of memory. Each beat of the clock pressed a leaden hand into his back, pushing him to face the single, cruel question that echoed in the marrow of his bones—how to cross the river of lies and step out, breathing, on the other shore. When the last light of the fire swallowed itself and the world was a circle of hush, he felt the ground beneath him shift. Retreat was not defeat nor was it flight; it was the hinge of fate, and he was the one who must turn it. Calling upon the calm that had seen him through other storms, he straightened to the night, slow and deliberate, ready to untie the riddle that curled like smoke around his heart.

In the frozen quiet of Siberia, where the wind told secrets and the nights were longer than regrets, Kofi learned to turn being alone into the brightest kind of light. Far from everything that had once crowded his life, he spread the empty space before him like an artist spreads fresh white snow, ready to write new stories over the old stains.

Lab lights washed the small room in icy white as Nova hunched over her workstation, a feverish calm wrapped around her. Her fingers danced over the keyboard, weaving impossible equations that tracked, traced, and predicted. At the same time, windows of data exploded across every screen, glowing like a storm of stars. Behind her, the drone of ventilators and the low pulse of processors beat like a heart that could not stop. Weeks had slipped by without a meal, without sleep, because the trace of the Russian Gambit still dangled before the world like a razor thread—lingering revelations that snipped at certainty and stitched fresh dread. Yet, buried inside the code, Nova sensed the first heat of a small flame. Slivers of the infinite data twined and folded, suddenly organised into a web too deliberate for chance. Events once scattered are now linked like fish in a line, their scales hiding markings only she could decipher. The awareness ignited her bloodstream—half triumph, half dread—while she pressed on, every keystroke vibrating with the promise that the answer lived just beyond the next threshold.

Nova felt the tremor of change in her fingertips and pressed on. The night hollered its hours, and still she laboured, her breakthrough sweating into shape, drawing her deeper into the heart of the Russian Gambit. Bit by bit, her ferret-bright research exposed the hidden net, a quiet ocean of zeros and ones spun to trap and rule. With every pulse, she followed the glimmering strands of the lie back to the womb, unrolling thread after thread of hush-script and spun-silence that the world had somehow missed. Code buttons clicked, hidden symbols glared, and each new mark dragged her nearer to the roaring centre. When dawn's first hush slid through the blinds, she felt it: the last symbol slid like a toad into its hole and the constellation snapped into focus. The revelation washed cold across her skin. The Russian Gambit had never been merely a chessboard of threats or bank-ruin; it was a scalpel of pure maths, polished to a cruel glint, like a prayer kept back from dawn, ready to carve chaos into every life that thrummed. The danger moved from thought to shape before her eyes. Heart pounding like a soldier's boot, she stepped from shadow to light. The signal had been born; the nations waited, and the first words on her lips would determine whether the blade sliced or was turned.

When the time came for Nova to present her findings to the world's most powerful leaders, she steadied her heart against the gathering storm. The Russian Gambit would storm into the light, its smiling mask ripped away. Because of Nova, nations would at last see the whole silhouette of the threat rising, dark and certain, against the skyline.

Inside the small Moscow office, bodies brushed past one another, the day's memory softened by cigarette smoke and machine hum. Nova perched over her screen, racing her pulse as she dragged millions of files into the light. Between the monitors, the silence was electric; every tremor of the keyboard felt like another heartbeat. The Gambit had taken a left turn none of them had seen, plunging them into a cave of secrets darker than they had pictured. Nova's fingers flew, but her stomach knotted further. They were no longer chasing maps or pixels; they were hunting stories. The numbers couldn't lie, but hearts and heads could be bent. The data could be polished into shields or sharpened into knives.

Omar huddled in the corner, slumped over the glowing screen, skimming through the unfiltered reports our field agents had just dropped. Knotted eyebrows, a steady jaw, the kind of quiet that screams. What his eyes showed was a steady rise in bad news and a churning clock. This wasn't analogue gambits anymore; the pieces were people, and a single slip meant more than a shattered file. Elena stood by the window, her back straight and her stare fixed miles beyond the skyline. She had long learned that in the high-stakes hush of our trade, colours bleed together until you can hardly find a true hue. Now that Nova had finally cracked the next layer of the matrix, we owed the operation more than metrics. We needed the edge that no algorithm could distil—hunch, muscle memory, that rare, bright flash of foresight that cuts through the static. One by one, the chatter of keyboards and quiet murmurs fell away until only the pulse of concentration thumped. Cameras, drones, chatter; we unspooled the thread of each pixel and blueprint, combing through slices of code and fishing for the whispered trails left by an unpredictable adversary.

Yet beneath the whirl of keyboards and buzzing wires, a calm certainty clung to the air. They were neither desk-bound analysts nor distant operators; they were warriors of thought, sworn to the silent war of images and stories, and they meant to prevail. Uncovering the naked truth was only the first half of the fight. The second, and the harder, half was to knead that truth into a tale that could cross borders, shatter minds, and bend belief to its will. As the clocks slipped toward another hour, the pressure pressed on them like a silent, iron shroud. The price of a single misstep had never been so cruel, and a creeping doubt darkened every choice. Yet the human heart remained the lodestar, a flickering lantern in the fog of fusion and false witness. When the growing weight threatened to crush their throats, they breathed the shared calm of each other's oath. The Russian Gambit had begun as a whispered grab for dominion; it had twisted into a collision of creeds, and they meant to conduct its final, definitive resolution.

As the world breathed faster and louder, Elena set out to shape a counter-narrative that would unseat the rising flood of certainty and doubt.

She dove into old archives and dusty files, finding tiny facts that looked ordinary at first but then began to fit together like a puzzle. Her careful work forced her to reconsider everything, urging her to wonder if they had ever zeroed in on the true danger. Uneasy feelings dogged her footsteps as she pulled the bright thread on a much darker scheme. By linking half-heard talk, ignored papers, and secret meetings, she followed a faint but exact line that threaded to a plot no one had dreamed could lie beneath the surface. The weight of what she found almost knocked the props from under the story that had guided every step they had taken. Her team loved the old story and brushed her ideas aside, but

Elena kept laying the proof in front of them one piece at a time. The papers were ordered, the logic tight, and slowly she breathed doubt into the air they had once taken for granted. Once-certain faces flickered, and the first dent in their certainty began to show.

After weeks of long nights dimmed by blue screens, Elena built a different set of facts, one that jolted the crew every time they reread it. Her numbers, her off-the-record leaks, and her gut-level hunches twisted the accepted story into a warning none of them had prepared for. When they finally sat together in the cramped conference room, her voice steady and her slides flashing, the room felt colder. Each slide peeled off the comfortable lies they had worn like armour, revealing a threat that had sprinted past their radar while they bickered over the obvious. The moment the last jab hit their faces, a cold charge of urgency surged through them. They understood: the danger didn't want them to see it coming, and it had dressed itself in the same red, white, and blue banners they'd trusted. They circled the table, swapping scepticism for resolve, and inked a new mantra on the whiteboard: Trust the pattern, not the noise. With every keystroke and every new file, they piled on the evidence that the danger was deeper, darker, and more agile than their worst-case screens had shown. The story they sensed in the hush of the mornings had now declared itself, and they were already sprinting towards the horizon, ready for the confrontation that would either expose the predator or consume them in the hunt.

Shrinking the distance to the truth, they peeled back the world's latest charades. Power had always masked itself with flags and slogans, but this time the husk of politics was only a very thin shell. Something colder and more personal loomed, not in headlines but in the silence of every forgotten table, every boardroom meeting judged too unimportant to record. The threat they felt now was not the roar of armies. Still, the hush of warehouses left unmonitored, of back doors in code that longtime insiders insisted on ignoring, and of graphs that flattened into lows no one was supposed to see. Human lives—ordinary, unguarded—were the variable, and whoever owned the variable owned the equation. The deeper they plunged, the more disgusted they became with the easy maps that had already failed them. There was no easy red line to follow, only dark points on a scatter they now had to trace by instinct. Trusting the hunch that had bitten them more than once, they divided the room. They started towards every low signal they'd once passed over, prepared to chase the shadow until it finally came into the light of their guns.

Nova stared at the piles of data, letting the numbers and the graphs spill across her mind like a deck of playing cards shuffling in a storm. She kept turning the same key until the lock fell open, only to find rust and more tumblers that quivered at her touch. Every time she tugged a thread, something blacker emerged from the weave, and she felt the chill of a warning that the game had escalated to something cosmic. This wasn't a scrap over kingdoms of land or sceptres of opinion; it was a siege against the heartbeat of the future. When that truth landed, it rattled her like a pebble in a glass house, shattering old mirrors. Somewhere in the dim corners, Elena spun her counter-narrative, layer on layer of sweet poison, and each statement went down like honey-coated shrapnel. She had tagged elites with silence and fogged the minds of seekers. Kofi had withdrawn, and the air felt too large without his pulse, like a drum mute on the last beat. Then, as if the universe had paused to listen, Nova's fingers brushed a data strand that glimmered ultramarine against the sepia of compromise. It was a long, fragile thread, but it was not knotted in despair. Still, the human factor loomed like a wild Rottweiler in a game of chess. Yesterday's champions had turned saboteurs, tomorrow's ghosts had become savours, and the alphabet of loyalty kept rescoring the same letters until each friend, without warning, could become the knife at the back.

The squad finally understood that danger did not reside in state capitals, but in singular souls who could rewrite tomorrow's headlines with a whisper. Steeling themselves, they prepared to face the approaching squall with the fierce promise to uncage the truth, whatever axe it swung. Yet, the trail before them would spiral into the epicentre of the grand trick, where solid ground turned to mist and reality wore the mask of a dream.

Shadows of the bunker pressed tight as Nova and her crew circulated over the tidal wave of raw code, the low hum of machines broken only by the rasp of breath. Days drifted away, coffee turned cold, but under their fevered squint, fractals first wiggled, then locked into sinister formation. The menace they had chased faded, a will-o'-the-wisp, and the real danger shifted like a black tide. Each line of ledger, each ajan of chatter, had a single signature sunk into it. Elena, the scarred historian of false tomorrows, dragged wicked birth-days and ghosted explosions out of archives, time-stamped lies scripted to mask the hand that first drew the blade.

Every shard of the puzzle locked into place with spooky precision, leading them past the enemy they had first named straight to the one they had overlooked. Morning light spilt through the window when Nova's thoughts finally quieted enough to count the implications. Unmasking the great deception, she realised, would need the lightest of hands; the truth they clutched could shatter the paper-thin balance holding nations apart. The moment the true architect caught the tiniest breath of their knowledge, the fallout could reach up to detonating missiles.

The team gathered, tight-faced, for an emergency council. Kofi, the diplomat with grey in his beard, urged caution, insisting they first weave an ironclad thread of proof. "A volley of noise, without the steel behind it, can ricochet back to us," he warned, his voice still calm. Across the table, Elena leaned forward, fire in her eyes. "Benching the truth is a gift to them. Each extra hour lets them dig deeper." Her knuckles were white on the metal surface, the difference between doubt and certainty pulsing in the dim light.

Amid the twisting doubts that surrounded her, Nova kept returning to the same quiet question, the one that kept her teammates whispering late into the night: Could they trust anyone who wasn't already family to them? Now that friend and enemy flickered like bad neon in the fog, every new alliance felt like a razor held to soft skin, and every tentative partner they approached carried the weight of hidden blades. Then, in a moment that felt both gift and curse, the Architect—a person every rumour painted as half ghost, half guardian—spoke in riddles. He dropped a name: the Unseen Grid. They say it pulses just beyond senses, its nodes guarded by ghost-light security, its agents moving like wind. Nova felt cold steel slide under her ribs; she and her team, just one name short of safety, had been dragged into the centre of the crossfire. Now the halls of power smelled of gunmetal and graft, and every doorway they passed glared with painted cameras. The burden pressed her shoulders into the earth. She stood in the middle of a grand lie. She understood that the choices stretched in front of her—some as simple as breath, others as heavy as storm—would decide whether tomorrow's sky held sunlight or ash. With the earth balanced on the tiniest edge, Nova gripped the century-old mission report now stained with her own sweat and stood, fists tight, ready to stare the coming night straight in the eye.

Chapter Five

The Architect

Around the long, polished table, the team leaned close, the room humming with nervous energy. They reviewed graphs, drone images, and chatter summaries, and the same daring idea gripped every mind. Nova had dropped a hunch last week, and ever since, every tiny detail had clicked into sharper focus. Together, they felt the team dynamic sharpen into a single blade of insight. What had seemed like scattered events now glimmered along a thin, unseen wire that only patience—and this moment—could expose. Guided by that wire, they ventured further into the funnel of numbers and shadows. Suddenly, fractals of meaning appeared in every nook. Attacks, tests, sabotage—spaced continents apart, yet rehearsed in the same awkward rhythm, staged by the same silent instructor. Coincidence fell away. Intent, slick and dark, revealed itself. The weight of the discovery settled like iron on their chests, and the room inhaled, waiting to breathe out the next question.

Nova spotted the pattern first. Her sharp eyes had always missed nothing, and this time they seized on the tiny details everyone else had let slide. While the rest of the team sifted through charts and logs, she leaned closer, circling the tiny overlaps and hinting that they were really the same pulse, the same thread, bending in disguise. The room fell quiet as they gathered around the screen. Nova sorted the tangle into columns of light and shadow, and in one stroke, the mystery grew a heartbeat. Kofi leaned back and stroked the scar on his cheek. Military order kicked in.

"Next, let's dig into the why," he said. "Every strike has a timeline, a message. The message is dust. What they really want is buried under the smoke. If we can smell the theatre, the puppeteer gets exposed."

The team nodded, suddenly aware that the brunt of the war was not in the wreckage but in the minds behind the wreckage. Elena, the code whisperer, had one more card.

The whiteboard was filled with numbers, traces, and cracked encryption.

"I peeled back the skin. There's a phantom backdoor I didn't know existed. Chasing it ends at a ghost site buried days deep and a handler I can't name."

Her voice crackled with the thrill of the impossible. The lights dimmed, and the room pulsed with the sense that the chase had just entered the open jaws of the labyrinth.

The new fragment lit up the darkness like a flare, revealing just enough of the shadowy builder behind the world's spinning disorder to turn the team's quiet wonder into loud, burning resolve. Watching the thin, shining shards of information click together, they felt the edge of discovery press against them like the cool side of a blade. Week after week, their late-night calls, their pushed coffee, their shared suspicions had turned into a durable shield. The theory they had hammered out, half-understood yet sturdy, now stood like a freshly drawn map, illuminated with the promise of the truth the storm had hidden. The moment felt like the moment before a dam breaks. Together, they moved toward the sound of rushing water, knowing they had to follow it to the water's final mirror, to the faceless builder who had dreamed of collapse and stop whatever shadow was already creeping up the other side.

While others debated the heartbeat of the new evidence, a quiet flicker inside Nova's mind widened into flame. Pattern and disorder were cousins she had stood with on late afternoons, and now, scanning the same columns of code, she caught a glimpse of broken symmetry. Kofi's sudden disappearing act was more than a clever retreat; it was the footprint of a clock that had been refastened to a different ring, a signal that something hidden had chosen to move.

The pieces of the puzzle fell into place, but none of them

looked the way she'd expected, and she alone could pry the door of the truth wide enough to slip through. Her thoughts fired like tiny rockets, streaking into constellations of theory and paradox, more elaborate and more precise with every heartbeat. Folders and hushed calls flew across the table as she laid her insight on the group, and soon their voices climbed to the ceiling like flames. The pressure of yesterday's horror pressed on their shoulders, yet Nova's flash of genius lifted them, thin as the first hint of dawn in the sky. For the first time, they could picture an escape route through the curtains of smoke, the tangled lies of an unseen enemy. With fresh purpose, they tightened their helmets. They stepped onto the wire, the knowledge that every inch of the coming ground could crack beneath them only sharpening the taste of the truth they could already taste.

The war room crackled with silence as shadows of generals carved the walls. Kofi eased back in the chair, the map's blue-grey light washing his face, and watched their raised voices like a film running too fast. Plans, counters, doubts, the night had ripped the mission, and now the only choice forged in his bones was a tactical retreat.

Kofi kept his eyes on the flat, careful faces around the table, and each one looked as if it carried the fate of the world on its shoulders. No one spoke of defeat, and yet not one of them could deny that everything hung by the thinnest thread. The voices across the room clashed and burned, yet Kofi stayed still, weighing the fury of each claim alongside maps that never stopped shifting in his mind. The possible futures rolled one after another, and he hunted for the one spark that could spark victory. At last, the chamber fell quiet, and he rose—not with volume but with presence. Every head turned. Kofi laid out a plan that stitched together every bead of his long service and stitched it with the enemy's patterns like a beadwork clasp. His reasoning sliced the arguments that still crackled like overheating wires. He spoke of the ruin that awaited a rush forward, and the silence that followed was not the hush of defeat but the hush of attention. Slowly, faces relaxed when the same truth crossed each mind. The same pencil that had marked every setback now traced the one red letter identifying their path. The call was written and sent: step back, step back. The energy in the room turned electric. Kofi drove himself into every detail of the retreat, folding the fire of every team into a single, steady fire. He reviewed each company's role, every order's clock, until the humming nerves of the men and women could beat as one.

His steady voice was like a chill wind turned warm; it settled the chatter of soldiers on the move, calming nerves even as the shell bursts drew closer. Kofi stood like a lighthouse while the ordered pull-back twisted through smoke, moving wounded and gear while the other side clawed at their backs. Every time the pursuers surged, Kofi adjusted the lines and kept men at their posts, folding fire from the hills into a tighter shield. By the time the last laggard passed the red tape marking safety, even the old carriers tipped their bore sights in salute. Kofi had seen the traps the scouts missed, had whispered the alternate streams of olive and steel, had turned panic into the metronome of retreat and turned retreat into breathing space. They had lost ground—temporarily, and at a cost of scars, not graves. The scout unit that night formed at dawn in the ruined meadow, rifles spattered yet singing, and the retreat was no longer a retreat; it was the nest a raptor builds before the drop.

Elena sat with the laptop open like a sleeping snake. Her fingertips were slick against the keys; the second password had slipped from her mind like a shell through a bolt. Outside, night folded over the shattered streets like a funeral shroud; the air tasted of burnt rubber and whispers. Thin light from the tiny safe house bled along the wall and bounced back from the kettle drum of the old wood stove, coarse and unmerciful.

Her heart thudded like a drum, every beat loud enough to drown out the rest of the world, while her brain scrambled to catch up. The task in front of her seemed impossible—she had to wade through oceans of data, tunnel through the maze of lies, and rip out the only piece of truth that might still be alive. Usually, she could climb out of her feelings and look at the numbers with a cold and steady eye. But now, under the bare light of her screen, the cold truth burned too hot to ignore. Panic climbed her spine. The files felt like a stone that only she was asked to carry, and she could almost hear the lives that hung in the balance, waiting for her to choose how to cut the thread. The deeper she went, the bigger the monster grew. The leak was rooted in the stone walls of the network itself, a worm eating the bones, showing wounds that no one had dared to touch. She stepped onto a knife's edge—stuffing the truth back in the box would mean slicing the trust she had sworn to protect and every line of her own code of honour.

Yet holding back the launch would gamble not just her own future, but the fragile lives of everyone she loved. Her gaze sped over the familiar tiles, searching for a trace of comfort. There was none, only the chill hand of duty. Seconds stalled, stretching into lifetimes, while she faced the weight of her choice. Finally, it was not bravery that pushed her, but a fierce refusal to let the shadows swallow them. With hands that shook from the storm inside, she typed a clipped command, dressing it in the last thin veil of trust. The coin was in the air, and its weight would jar every knot of friend and foe. The board had changed, and the game was only starting.

When the last dust settled and the heavy echo of treachery filled every corner, Nova's calm mask broke just a crack. A bitter spark of audacity crackled in the room. At the same time, Kofi fought to untangle the poisonous threads of Elena's leaked design. The silent, accusing looks that passed among the team murmured a single, stunned thought: none had seen this blow coming.

Every single member of the Spectre Squad had been grilled to the marrow, their loyalties pulled apart under the harshest light, leaving the tiniest crack an open doorway. Yet now they sat inside the chill puppet theatre of an unknown master, strings humming under the skin. Silence is narrow enough to slice. Nova lifted her eyes, a still fire, and held every gaze one heartbeat longer, masking the one crack in her armour—a crack that showed anyone unafraid of the dark where the light leaks in. She knew. Elena's whispers had dug up the past the squad had buried long ago, and those hollow rooms thundered in the now.

When the moment came, a ghost of a moment, Nova peeled back the sheeting years. The numbers and the subpoenas had been her carapace, hiding the cuts and stitches a thousand problem-gamers had turned into sinew. Brutal calibration of every puzzle breathed truth into her fingers and left her eyes shielded. The shards she laid before them fused into the only cable left unsevered—hers pressed to the wound they now lived in. And then the curtain dropped. The interior foe they had sworn to crush was already in the marrow of the squad—an artist of betrayal who chalked their every heartbeat on a ledger of sinew and bone. The ring of shattered trust chimed like a countdown; they gripped the table, knuckles white, and the sharp smell of fighting back filled the room.

The crew moved with cold, careful precision, hunting vengeance with every heartbeat. First, they counted what they had—files, wires, faces that could still be trusted—then quietly traced paths off the map, clicking darkened doors open, each step a tile laid on the road to the architect's name. What they could not see was the curtain the architect had woven day by day, was fraying—dropped threads that shone like ink on glass—leading straight to a confrontation the streets had not yet whispered. Doubt crept like fog, but doubt was not more substantial than the spark, so they laced their boots, strapped on the lies that kept them breathing, and stepped into the smoke once more. Mirrors would shatter, masks would bleed, and the farther they moved into the maze, the less the distance to the answer mattered. The answer itself would stretch beyond any map they could fold.

Nova had always been a riddle wrapped in a cloak of smoke. She had arrived in their lives quietly, the key to her beginning forgotten between the pages of a much-read book. No one understood the story of where she had come from, and no one had ever pressed the question too far. Those who probed the edges of her memory were caught in a snare of half-concealed truths and false trails, unable to keep their footing. Yet for Kofi and Elena, the need for the whole tale had turned urgent, because the next dawn might demand more from them than they were ready to give. While the others circled the puzzle, they chose to walk deeper into the shadowed corridors of her yesterday. They found, to their astonishment, a life stitched with contradictions. Nova had once sat beneath the flickering light of candle and star, studying vanished kingdoms, forgetting dreams, and the slender logic that some call magic. Her thirst for knowledge had never respected walls, spilling her first into libraries and then into darker vaults where lanterns burned with an unkind light. Rumour had painted her first as a student of fallen wisdom, then as the first candle of a distant dawn. With every piece Kofi and Elena turned, they met encounters that laughed at reason and slid like quicksilver through the sieve of logic.

The pathway wound through hidden libraries, moss-covered monasteries, and secret leagues, each site delivering riddles wrapped in dust and silence. Stories of sunken empires, vanished tribes, and banned scriptures whispered of a hidden purpose weaving through Nova's silent mask. Each cough of new evidence let Kofi and Elena peer a little deeper into a mind that mocked easy labels. Her past stretched like a reclaimed manuscript, layers of vanished ink, half-faded truths, and stubborn contradictions that stretched their perceptions and bent their endurance. The more they sifted through Nova's yesterday, the more their own cracks widened, because the darkness of her yesterday kept spilling into their now. With every secret pulled from the archives, the outline of her history sharpened, and a chill thread of doubt snaked through the uncertain tomorrow they once believed they could steer.

After Kofi withdrew under fire, the intelligence circles crackled like exposed wire. Nova's tangled biography now hovered like a ghost above their maps. With the shards finally locking, it was plain they confronted a new kind of foe—one that redefined what defeat might look like the moment it entered their lives.

What they uncovered sent chills through the room. This was not a test of cleverness any more; it was a gamble that could tip the whole world. The Architect's twisted design had caught them in a fold they could not escape, one tiny mistake away from everything shattering. While they scrambled for the next possible counter, rumours of a traitor hidden among them pushed the air tighter. Seconds stretched like hours, every tick a reminder that they stood on the lip of the void, one slip from oblivion. Under the weight, friendships cracked, vows vanished. The ground they thought solid twisted like exposed roots, and the only thing sure was that nothing was certain. Each exposure of truth turned comrades into possible saboteurs, and the trail ahead was swallowed in shadow.

The Architect had pushed a boundary none of them had sensed, and the danger no longer wore a single flag. It rolled past borders, past creeds, past raised hands that had once been shoulder to shoulder. If they faltered, it was not defeat—it was erasure. The team steadied for whatever storm was next, hearts armoured with the knowledge that the cost of losing was everything.

This wasn't just another mission any more; it had turned into a battle for survival against an enemy who turned knowledge into the sharpest sword. With cold-eyed focus, they loaded up for the new front, counting every scrap of gear, every shard of data, every ounce of grit they could summon. The Architect had created a grand stage of lies and puppet strings, and they were walking on that stage with nothing but iron will and the fiery conviction that the truth would rise in the end.

Against the skyline of a city ready to topple, Nova and her squad stepped into a gamble where hope and terror had merged into a single heartbeat. Winding through the enemy's underbelly, they began to feel the tight, slick strands of the trap coiling around their ankles. Every door they pushed open, every relay of code they breached, tightened the noose an inch farther. Whatever creature hunted them in the dark, it moved without sound, without scent, and yet it knew every heartbeat. Still, the team pressed forward, throats dry and pulses loud, knowing that one slip could darken the sky in a single blink.

The city throbbed like a wound, bracing for a blow no one could see. Responsibility sat like iron on their chests. Every ticking second dragged them deeper into the puzzle, where danger flinched beneath every streetlamp and hid in the lilting rise of a stranger's voice. While the air still crackled, Elena caught a half-erased scrawl in a ruined doorway—words, numbers, symbols, breathing a warning that tugged them toward a secret that could break or make them. Whoever spun this night had already played every possible hand, turning the skyline into a chessboard. In this maze, even the rain felt like a whispered lie.

Nova's mind raced against the blur, turning each erratic clue into a possible bridge. The riddle coiled tighter—one red herring followed by another—yet gradually the thorns slid into alignment, and a sliver of daylight cut the darkness. That fragile light sparkled like a match caught in the wind, and the team huddled close, ready to light their way through the enemy's mind-bending snare. Just as they dared to think they had gained the upper hand, betrayal exploded in their faces like glass. The move had been surgical, breathtaking, and it splintered the delicate string of trust that had kept them standing.

The first shock still shook them when the next blew in like a gust that froze the blood. They stood on a ledge above darkness, and in that still, quiet heart of the nightmare, they understood: the real test was finally rolling toward them. Its weight would crush them, or exalt them, and it carried the slender hope of the city on its back.

Across every quiet screen where the watchers usually fidgeted, the fading hush of the first eruption snapped back to life. Fear, thin and cold, slid like a blade through every agency. They all felt it—this was not the finish; it was the ominous horizon before the storm. Behind locked doors and in forgotten rooms, minds older than maps strained to find the trail, to guess the moving shadow, to plant the first tiny shoot of hope before a new rupture tore it away. The enemy, a phantom that thought in numbers and darkness, had invented a danger smarter than any they had known. Chasing every slender thread they uncovered led only to new, branching knots. Nova, Kofi, and Elena stood shoulder to shoulder in the eye of that twisting wind; each wore a private wound, each lifted the other's weight even as they fought not to fall. The game had deepened; they had no choice but to deepen with it.

All across the ether, colours flickered and shadows stretched, giving everything the wrong angle. Friendships and betrayals weighed the same. Redemption, once a bright promise, is now a heavy stone in their packs. Helicopters of code whirred overhead, and everyone sensed the chill: the coming blow wasn't just a missile punch. It was a song of ruin, note by note, designed to unravel borders and burn the ink of treaties and make even silence scream for the end. A hollow beep, a red flash, the second pulse ticked toward midnight, and the skyline of tomorrow teetered on a single, fraying wire. The arena was no arena. It stretched into the skin of the street and the zeroes of the grid, where a finger on glass could tip the world forward or fade it to black. The master-crafters of the ruin sharpened their keys, ready to smear the white page of history with a cruelty no storyteller could ever erase. The hush was a tightening noose, because once the hush broke and the second pulse flew, roads would fracture, choices would burn, and never would any traveller find their way back.

When the din of the second pulse finally quieted, a white scar across the skyline, someone exhaled like it was the first breath of a newborn world. The net crackled with whispered prayers and curses, while the rubble of a skyline flickered like a vanished dream. The horizon still blinked and throbbed, echoing the last note of the ruins.

The game inside the game had begun, each player pushing the board's corners with deliberate, quiet force. They knew, now, that the round had grown larger than themselves: decisions whispered in high towers bounced down alleyway marketplaces, rippling outward. It felt, for the first time, as if the world had peeled back a skin to expose the moving strands of falsehood hiding under the skin of every day. Centred in the widening circle stood Nova, her green gaze lit from within, fierce enough to burn through the dark. She believed, with a clarity that thundered, that she alone carried the answer sealed inside the unfolding riddle. The board itself widened with every heartbeat, welcoming gullible corners and hardened veterans in one pull. Kofi, eyes calm as a still lake, prepared a daring stroke that would gamble every bond of faith. Elena, undeterred, plotted a treacherous course through the twisting tunnels of half-truths. Then the Architect slipped from dusk, cornered the silence, and began measuring every clang of confusion as if with musical notation. The first deliberate glide of a piece had already skidded forward, and the trajectory now promised to redraw the map of every realm.

On the chill breeze, the name Meridian drifted like a half-remembered dream, ringing with the weight of old prophecies that had once ruled the world but now served only to chill the marrow. Nations tilted close, then pulled apart; daggered words turned to bonds of steel, and the court whispered that the wheel had begun to spin. Invisible hands knotted the fates, threading the night with the colours of panic and hope alike. At the centre, where night and wind conspired, a single phrase budged against the roof of every mind: the ending had no clear shape, for the rules were blades and the hourglass was always half-emptied. The first piece had moved, and with that step, every heart, every crown, every hidden name was locked into the same, dark promise.

Part Two: The Global Gambit

Chapter One

The Asian Blackout

The skyline of Singapore went black all at once, the city's lights extinguished as if the universe had drawn a cosmic breath. The streets beneath went quiet, the usual whirl of motors, chatter, and lifts pausing in an unsettling hush that pressed against the towers like a held note. In the middle of the hush, Omar stood alone in his office, silhouetted against the greying blinds, the moon scraping a cold silver across his cheekbones. The darkness outside curled in at the window like liquid shadow, asking questions for which he had no easy answer.

While the streets flared with startled faces and sirens, his small glass room remained a fortress of calm. He had rehearsed this moment, and the quiet blue light of a single, protected server in the corner kept whispering the numbers and maps that the blackout had tried to drown. Every red dot flashing across the digital display reminded him of how small certainties could become potent weapons. The data granted him a grip that felt like warmth against the cold of unknown hours, and he savoured its weight.

Messages crawled in from his nested cells: lifts pinned, traffic grids choke-pointed, feed nets going dim. The city of tomorrow could still be coaxed to breathe according to a preview he alone had sketched. Omar combed through the text, his heartbeat synchronised to the metronome of probabilities and contingent plans dancing behind his narrow eyes. He felt the darkness stretching across the bay, a question mark for anyone who wondered what sort of night it had become.

The blackout had not descended by coincidence. Omar could sense, in the chill that crept along his spine, the fingerprints of intent. Network after network had flat-lined in perfect synchrony, each pulse of the grid disappearing as if filtered by invisible fingers. The impossibility of the hour—just beyond the last relief shift—told him that the hand was human, though the grasp was cold. Rather than cower in the velvet blackout, he welcomed its cavern, his mind already picking through the fragments of the shattered night.

The city had always worn its light like a living medal that swallowed the sun. Now that the medal dulled, and with the dullness came the howl of hundreds of thousands of private storms, each one a room turned feverish with the aftershock of a power cut. Omar thought of the neon letters that had blinked above the taxis, of children clinging to the glow of failed tablets, of security stations bright with doubt. The city had a heartbeat; now, that heartbeat flickered, and he could feel the pulse of every suppression he had ever learned to ignore. Yet he would not bend to the hush. Forces dark and hidden had thrown the dice, but Omar would lift the cup, heedless of how many times they had struck against him. The whole constellation of the skyline needed him, the arteries of the undersea cables needed him, the humming lacquer of the MRT needed him. Years of night-walks through humming converter stations coursed through his mind like a song.

He swore to himself—no one would die locked against the night. The towers could spill their light again, and he would light them with the truth of the men who had turned their backs. Every nerve tightened. He welcomed the ache. He would cut through the dark and find the actor behind the mask. Even if the answer breathed poison, Omar was already turning toward the heart of the city, a small ember of absolute certainty warming his chest in the velvet chill. In that narrow, barely buzzing room, he sat absolute as a prayer, spine unyielding against the night, eyes locked against the place where the skyline should be.

When the whole city dropped into darkness, he felt the certainty that panic was coming, like an animal that scents blood. The week's unravelling events flickered through his mind, each one stranger and more trouble-breeding than the last. He had always thought of himself as a creature of reason, confident that reason and a trained gut could steer him through the shadowy alleys of international politics. Now, the whole machine refused to work. For the first time in memory, doubt thick and wet like fog choked the edges of his thought. The cool, iron spine of his will bent for a heartbeat as he faced the scale of the breakdown. The daily, predictable politics that soothed him every sunrise had frayed and dropped away, leaving him dangling in a spider's lace of falsehood and peril.

He studied the blackout, heart pounding with the march of time, and traced each possible interpretation like a thin crack spreading in glass. How could so much grid flicker down and stay down without a whisper of warning, without a likely explanation? What buried hand had pressed the lever? He had survived mutiny in small states, plebiscites gone feral, and sanctions that turned neighbours into strangers, but none of those storms tasted like the present one.

As was his habit after sunset, Omar's memory replayed the hushed voices he'd caught slipping through the alley gates, the quiet exchanges no louder than smoke, and the gnawing fear that he'd stepped without knowing onto a faded game board where none of the pieces belonged to him. He pushed away from the cracked window, letting the chill mist of the city's ruin crawl over his hands. He would go deeper, peel back the layers of lies, the misdirections layered like cheap paint over rotten wood, until the heart of the shadow was bare and beating under his palm. Facing his own pale mirror, he felt the embers of refusal flare and settle, a quiet fire vowing to lift the masks from the true faces of the night and keep the tremulous balance the world still, absurdly, prayed to keep.

Silicon City had bent and broken, the skyline swallowed by the same moonlight that no longer felt romantic but feral. Black tides had crept through the neon veins, infecting the pulse of the city until the hum of power faded to silence. Train lines shuddered to a crawl, streetlamps blinked one last cold goodbye, and the low thrum of the crowd fell silent, as if the city had taken a shuddering breath and forgotten the exhalation. Voices had vanished into the crackling air, safety SMS pregnant with static, and the sky above lay like an un-blinking eye. The strike had the precision of a surgeon's knife and the cruelty of a storm, and its aftertaste sent ripples of fear across borders. Nations bent low over glowing screens, fingers flying, the seconds counting louder than any siren, the hunt for the blackout's architects just a breath before midnight.

Amid rising chaos, lonesome analysts dashed through darkened lane-ways of coding. Under the red glare of bro-ken displays, fingers danced like frantic drummers, tracing digital blood trails back to the shadowed architects. Every keystroke, every stale subroutine whispered fatal details. Master cyber-sleuths—silicon-wizards trained for the impos-sible—sprinted through seven virtual vaults, probing the meat-layer of the superconducting city turned ghost. Above, CCTV cameras turned blank—red light blinking slowly, like the heartbeat of the night. Kofi, formerly of the neon-lit gun-boat team, now wore the city's sirens like a bone-cut tattoo. Under a black hoodie, he turned alley-echoes into breathing maps, sliding through choke-points even station rats knew. But the puppeteer danced six moves ahead, every safe route now laced with double-vision traps. So Kofi pivoted into a dark web of flickering chat rooms, where dog-faced avatars hissed fractured truths: the ghost wants blood, not data.

Daruma dolls ate the neon rain behind him as the last ghost of the doughnut shop's fried-squid scent faded. Kofi felt the lacquered soles of shadow cops crack on distant pavements, a subtle countdown he had learned to read like a heartbeat. Through the satin drizzle, Faith said the Cy-press Church's firewall loved him back. Tonight, digital gods whispered of subnet cathedrals where even the dead could breathe a bit longer.

The city's digital nightmare gripped every corner, and Kofi moved like a whispered prayer: light, then shadow. He carried secrets heavier than iron, and the ones who'd snuffed the screens now hunted his footsteps. He darted between puddles of sickly light and the gusting wind, his mind a storm of questions. Who still walked beside him? Where, inside a city folding in on itself, could a red thread of safety be tied? Solace flickered in the belief one heart, somewhere, still burned for the truth he carried.

The night air curled like smoke, sharp with warning. Each ticking second tightened the noose and drew him nearer to the dark heart of the blackout. Duty and the stubborn prayer that history might one day read his name pushed him forward. He could hear his heart banging against his ribs, a twin revolt to the silent city. Betrayal draped a thin grey cloak across his shoulders, yet the ember behind his ribs flared brighter. With every hushed footfall, Kofi chose truth over the silent grave they offered him, and for that, he chose to keep running.

With every footfall, Kofi promised himself he would stay one step ahead, prove his innocence, and expose the shadowy forces he could barely name. Slipping beneath the spreading arms of an ancient temple, he caught his breath and planned his escape. Fear squeezed him like a belt, but he pushed back with a steadiness that could only come from having nothing left to lose. A faint rustle broke the stillness, and the surge of adrenaline turned his heart to fire. He slid into a crouch, poised to vanish or to fight, every move honed by months of flight. Tightening the braid that had become his only anchor, he locked his gaze past the cracked pillars, carrying the weight of secrets he should never have uncovered and a faith that would not let him yield. Unbeknownst to him, the universe had already rolled the dice, pointing him toward an ally he would never have chosen yet would soon find he could not survive without.

Elena stood where the slick pavement split the city like a scar, torn between the badge she had sworn to and the conscience that had never let her sleep. The skyline flickered like an agitated heartbeat, the neon promises of a broken night exploding around her. She could hear the sirens, distant yet crying, like a child that would not hush; she could smell the smoke and the jasmine from the vendors. Across the river, lights pulsed in a rhythm she knew was not celebration. In that noise, the truth knocked, asking whether a good soldier could be a good human, even if her orders smelled like ash.

The city lurched towards disaster, the way a tightrope snaps when the last spar breaks. Elena's hands shook around the file, wires at the spine pinched like live coals. Inside, theories and coordinates could redraw every frontier, every alliance. She had spent the last five years obeying the voice in the dark, a master swallowed by rumours, whose orders slipped like mercury into phones, back doors, and boardrooms.

The first taste had been pure crystal—money, access, the brush of power across her skin. Now the taste rotted under her tongue. The knowledge that she had nudged the world closer to a staged, simulated war gnawed like acid. A deep, sour disappointment rose, swelling to her throat. She had believed she was stacking chips in a high-stakes game; now she saw the table was a slaughterhouse. Still, a small ember smouldered beneath the ash: a stubborn, salt-and-earth belief that the arc of a shattered life could reset if a hand was steady enough to withdraw. Croft's name lingered through her thoughts like a closed door slamming. He appeared at the top of every door-sequence in her memory, voice a velvet blade, smile an election onto her better nature. Above him, the unspooled heavens rattled, perhaps waiting for her to let go and fall, possibly cheering for a swing back, a retake.

With the truth about him locked inside her mind, Elena stood at the edge of a choice so sharp it felt like glass against her skin. She could keep pretending to serve him, or she could step off the cliff and find answers the world wasn't ready to hear. The city outside her window throbbed like a giant heart, and every thump slid through her ribs, daring her to follow it. Minutes slipped through her fingers like smoke, while dark omens gathered at the city gates, whispering that her courage wasn't enough. Alone in the searing hush, she felt every possible outcome ripple out, a million lives dangling on the single word she had to say next. She could almost hear the crowds counting on her, and for the first time, it felt like she was counting on herself.

Deep in the twilight office of Croft International, an electric stillness wrapped itself around the room. The sinking sun slashed red streaks against the glass, and Markus Croft leaned behind his massive mahogany desk, fingers locked in front of his mouth. The weight pressing down felt darker than night; his ultimatum was a silent thunderclap. One more word, one sharp ring from the desk phone, and the subtle balance of an entire continent would tip the wrong way. He was the one holding the joker, the spade, and the ace. Across the floor, Kofi Nyarko stood like a statue, shoulders tight, knowing whatever Croft said next would be chiselled into every textbook yet to be printed. Croft, sinking deeper into the worn-leather chair, felt the old fatigue fold new lines into his face; every wrinkle a reminder of lost sleep, of old fights. The price of his choice was an open sea, and yet the call to see justice swim back to shore held him steady. The desk drooped under the weight of gilt and glass—a delicate cut-crystal decanter, amber liquid swimming like slow confession under the pale shimmer.

With careful calm, Croft poured two healthy drams of the decade-old whisky, a quiet salute to the heaviness of the talk to come. He lifted the glass, tasted the smoky burn, then settled his sharp gaze on Kofi, who answered with steady eyes of his own. Both men knew the moment rippled far beyond politics or power; it reached straight into the heart of freedom and conscience. As the fire of the liquor settled in his chest, Croft felt the tangling threads of his own dark tunnel. The search for justice had hurled them to this fracture, and the past had already slipped away. He set the crystal down, folded his hands, and leaned close, his cold look drilling into Kofi. In a voice that forgot the meaning of debate, he drew the line that could not budge. Every syllable thrummed with the echo of a thousand fought-for truths, a thousand oaths. Kofi weighed the finality of the offer, aware that the road stretching ahead was strewn with shadows sharper than blades.

The fading light pooled like smoke in the corners of the room, lengthening every shadow until they felt like doubt dragging at their heels. Outside, the world itself wavered, and Croft's single, cold order had swung the balance. His final words, brittle yet final, had dwindled to nothing, but the silence that followed rang louder than any roar. They had rolled the dice now, and both could feel the hard truth—no way to wager or regret what came next. Every choice they made would race across oceans, and soon the globe would tremble with the tremor they had only seen glimmering at the far rim of the night. In that hush, the fate of entire nations dangled, shaking, until the clock chose to strike on Croft's ultimatum.

The air felt steeped in electrostatic dread as the team gathered at the scarred map table, tense and pale. The projection hummed to life, spilling green light across their faces and showing a frantic lattice of relay towers and spinning cypher rings. Hour by hour, the chart brightened, and at last a malignant geometry swam into focus: a lattice of lies, tightening like a noose. The sting of it landed cold in their bellies—they were not the masters of their own fight. Still, bones rolling in a game clawed by a nameless hand long hidden, yet every fingertip stretched to every sky.

Every step they took had been calculated before they even decided to take it, and every counter they threw had been met before it started to fly. Now they hung, weightless, before an enemy they could not see. The magnitude slammed against them, twisting their mission into a black question mark and stretching the enemy's hands farther than they had ever imagined. It was Kofi, as always, who felt the slight shiver in the stream.

Following a string of digital crumbs, he stumbled into the last place he ever expected—one of their own. The revelation sliced through them like cold steel. Friends suddenly carried the cilantro of doubt, and comrades avoided even casual glances. The air in the safe room buzzed with a static the fans could not clear; loyalties were magnets flipped in an instant. Elena, calm as the eye of the storm, scanned the data again, her gaze a lighthouse the darkness could not extinguish. Omar stood a step apart, the old oath and the new price twisting in his head, the truth that the rot had fed on their own soil gnawing at his every breath. In that narrow, charged silence, they leaned together and whispered their next move, folding every syllable into the shape of a plan. Decisions hung above them like a storm cloud, and the shape of Meridian's purpose loomed just behind it, pushing them edgeward, pushing them forward.

As each dark fragment clicked into the larger picture, the team steadied themselves for what was coming next, aware that the reveal of the Shadow Collaborator was merely the flimsy cover of a storm bigger than any of them had imagined, a storm that might drown the world in chaos.

The overhead bulbs flickered like dying stars, dripping their cold light into the narrow alley where Croft walked, footfall quiet, heartbeat loud enough to drown a shout. Every sense buzzed, on fire with a warning he could not ignore. A string of anonymous texts had come to his phone, each line more jagged than the last, each line telling him to keep this midnight hour—and this hidden place—open for the one person who carried the truth about Meridian's buried design. Crouched candle-high against the wall, he counted his last steps. Then a shape melted from the deeper darkness, enough of a person to block the light but not enough to give a name.

The voice that cut the air was a blade: thin, thrumming, frightened enough to curdle the chill. The urgency in it was like a brand on his skin, warning he had seconds left to believe. Whoever this was had already walked miles too far, had already tasted the weakest blood of secrets that could give or take a nation. The collaborator's words spilt in short, jagged bursts, each one a shard of ice: Meridian's hidden plans, the data farms buried under half a continent, the back doors already in the halls of generals—everything strung together like bones in a hundred small, invisible puppets. The picture that rose from those bones was cold and clear: a global net closing, the last moment to cut the wires humming louder than any fire alarm.

When the words finally hit him, Croft felt cold creep up the back of his neck. This news was bigger than borders and money—bigger than empires—because it reached inside everyday lives and tried to rewrite them. The hush of the hidden meeting spilt secret after secret, and the inside man's voice pulsed with something heavier than fear. It was guilt, the kind that chases you long after the crime, and remorse that burns every time you remember you (for a long time) helped the very thing you now want to destroy. Croft felt the urge to reach through the dark and squeeze that trembling hand, to say:

"You aren't alone, not now."

Then the room tilted. A cold, brittle truth cut through: the watchers were already in the shadows, breath steady and cameras rolling, ready to erase the fragile light they'd just kindled. Loyalty in a place like this was a page that turned the instant you stopped looking at it. The inside man risked every secret and every breath to rip that page out, to shout truth into the storm, to say once and for all that black silence would not be the last word.

When the last echoes of the confrontation faded, Croft made a silent promise to guard this unexpected comrade, to plunge deeper into the twisting tunnels of lies and puppetry surrounding the crimson logo of Meridian. The price of failure loomed larger than ever, the obstacles more brutal, yet a little flame of determination flared within him. Because in the thick night of coming danger, they had forged a bond nobody had foreseen. This bond might finally shred the mask from Meridian's poisonous face.

When the world's watchtowers finally glimpsed Meridian's real face, a cold tremor ran through every vault of secrets and every shielded citadel of the globe. Threads of falsehoods peeled away, and every analyst, every sentry, understood that Meridian was far more than another brood of mercenary ghosts spreading ruin for coins or crowns. Its manoeuvres, tangled and concealed in shadow, bowed not to greed but to a doctrine colder than ice. This doctrine placed the doctrine itself above flesh and coin. Old echoes—the forgotten sabotage, the whispered disappearances—locked together like teeth on a gear, and the grinding teeth whispered the same terrible design slowly completed across scarred years. The mask of a benign data empire shattered, leaving only a slow, pitiless thrum where mercy had seemed to dwell.

At the centre of this dark design hovered a quiet ring of schemers, each feeding secret dreams of control and darkness. They had twisted every gadget, counted every ally, and drained every asset to trigger a disaster that would ignite their ruinous order. Their shadowy grip whispered into the boardrooms of presidents, into the vaults of bankers. Among the codes of armies, wrapping unwitting pieces into a chess game, no player could quit. With surgical craft, they had planted seeds of hatred and suspicion, watering ruin and confusion in darkened rooms while smiling in the daylight.

When the truth pierced the rose-coloured fog and revealed that Meridian was no mere grab for power or riches, but a drive to cage the human heart and bind it under a god-like master, dread settled like ice in the marrow of the few who could read the magnitude of the storm. They knew: the cost of failure soared; the hourglass drained. While whispers of revolt gained volume and every number, every gun, and every heartbeat fell into position, the ticking clock turned into a drum. The fight had narrowed to a sprint against the dark.

Every clue, every whispered secret, and every shadowy mission spun together in a last-ditch push to tear apart the big cover-up and stop the disaster that was already creeping closer. For the first time, the planet stood eye to eye with an enemy whose dreams stretched to every horizon and whose cruelty came without a second thought. Light and dark were about to collide, and the survival of every human being hung in the balance.

The moment Meridian's actual game was unmasked, a surge of urgency jolted the team. The weight of that secret group's deadly power settled over every continent like a dark cloud. Seconds were slipping away, the pressure surged, and every heartbeat turned into a race. Knowing that the truth could tilt the balance of everything, every member dug in with a fierce, unyielding resolve. They were driven by the fierce duty to lay the secret bare. The countdown was anchored in a cold, careful plan to strip away every fake mask Meridian had grown around its hidden deeds. Under the brutal glare of what was at stake, friendships were strained, and the shadow of double-cross hung in every corner, ready to blow their carefully laid plans to dust.

Across borders, quiet missions unfolded with calm certainty, each member slipping through clouds of deception planted by their shadowy foe. Every action carried the weight of worlds, teetering just beyond the edge of a truth the globe could hardly bear. Inside this perilous game, the ticking clock toward exposure transformed itself into a single cry for justice and honesty, a rising chorus of calculated decisions racing towards one moment that would turn the arc of history itself. Steeled against whispers of doubt and the hardest of trials, the crew stood shoulder to shoulder, their loyalty a shield against panic. Piece by piece, the truth that had once flittered just beyond their fingertips came into view, a fragile star against the dark. With the last seconds slipping away, they breathed the same tense air, a quiet roar carried by hearts that had never learned to cower. The previous seconds glimmered like struck flint, ready to blaze through nights of cunning, to reveal a world that had cowered in silence for far too long.

Chapter Two

The UN Insider

Lena Petrov was a riddle dressed like a devoted diplomat. Raised in a family famed for devotion to duty, she grew up breathing the old rule that privilege carries responsibility. Even as a child, her mind was like a bright compass pointing toward a better world. At the world's best schools, she absorbed everything that could sharpen her for the art of nations. She climbed the UN ladder with a speed that startled old hands, earning both medals and grudging respect. But somewhere in those dizzy heights, other ideas slipped inside her—ideas that taught her to dream of a single, strong world government free of the old bonds of borders and flags.

We quietly started retracing her steps. The more we dug, the more her life read like a book of changes, each chapter bending her from honourable advice to a fierce, singular dream. The UN still had her body, but a deeper loyalty had claimed her heart, one that discarded familiar gods of country and conscience in favour of a shimmering, uncertain promise.

With every secret move she made, it was clear that Lena had a knack for bending her private goals into the design of something darker and wider. She was changing, and we had to watch hard, for what had looked like a calm push for world unity now showed a hidden pact ready to shake the very bones of global order. Our squad understood that mapping Lena Petrov's past and present was the key to unravelling the fine threads of lies and control we were tracing through several continents and clashing creeds. Only by following her would we find the centre of the long, quiet game threatening to explode into daylight.

While the first light poured over Manhattan, Elena Petrov slid into her favourite navy suit, the one she trusted for both tense boardrooms and secretive nighttime runs. Slipping the silk scarf into place, she let the sharp chill seep into her bones and trained her watchful blue gaze on the UN dome, the black ice-water tower framing the morning. Inside, Kofi Adewale, the diplomat everyone respected and nobody really knew, was perfecting the script for a final draft that might tear borders apart and redraw oceans. Every fibre in her drove her forward.

Months before, a failing mic in Kigali, a tossed note in Brussels, and a blurred drone scan over the desert had whispered the first syllables of his name into her ear. Elena had pocketed each fragment—Russian scans, Chinese scans, one riddle tucked in a gold folder in a tower bathroom—and built the puzzle inside her head. Kofi was both the signature and the lock on a global secret that smelled too much like the last century's ghosts. Bit by bit, she had reached the centre, but he had peeled away like a magician's last silk ribbon, making her question if she had ever really had him at all. Every stride forward pressed a fresh bruise of accountability into her ribs. The balance never tipped; the scales refused mercy. From the winding boulevards of Paris to the candlelit halls of the Saudi guard, she had hounded the thin outline of his back—always a heartbeat, a Jetstream, a name away.

But today, when the first light streaked the dawn, Elena felt the whole game pivot underneath her. She descended the ramp into the underground garage, slid into her matte-black saloon, and felt the leather wheel bite into her palms above the steady pulse of her own heart. She ghosted through the concrete canyons, skipping between parked cars and pillars as if they were lasers in a tight security drill, her mind unloading a thousand scripts and backup scripts faster than her breath. When the garage doors hissed open and Midtown's blur of horns and headlights hit her, Elena measured the humid air and tasted risk. Salvation and catastrophe were the same breath away.

At the same hour, Kofi was already in motion. Locked into the echoing corridors of the UN tower, he felt the building shudder with new whispers. Rumours spun like loose wires—clandestine dinners, sealed lifts, and favours traded beneath the fluorescent glare. He breathed slower, still tasting yesterday's coffee, and let the rising static in his gut sharpen into focus. This was, he felt, the moment he had rehearsed while staring through his own reflection. Pressing the polished key card to the scanner, he reminded himself: the man he would face inside had the password to everything, the moment the world still called peace. Kofi stepped through the clicking turnstile and into the lion's den, palms damp but hands steady.

He could feel the weight of danger closing in on him like a wet blanket—multitudes of hidden hands pushing him toward a cliff. His heartbeat drummed images of Lena Petrov into his skull. Even her name smelled like smoke; he didn't know what fire she meant to start, but he was certain he could not stick around to watch it spread. Footfalls barely a whisper on the cold floor, he ghosted along the dim corridors, nerves bursting like dry leaves. Any flicker, any breath of air across his skin, sent his spine into a shiver. For a flickering breath, he dared to convince himself he was alone, but the taste of watchful eyes slid like ice between his ribs. Then a dull silver line caught his gaze—a service door, barely open, the dark beyond it breathing in his direction. Courage kicked him in the gut, and he propelled himself forward, through the narrow gap, into a service corridor that exhaled the sour memory of grease and rust. He was not safe yet.

An array of security gates rose like sentinels, each red-lit eye a razor blade across his plan. Kofi planted his feet, drumming his fingers against the rough metal, calculating every breath. Leaving behind the hushed corridors that had grown old along with secrets, he squared his shoulders and summoned the memory of wind on wide open fields, cholera-free and empty of shadows.

Kofi leaned on everything he'd ever learned about talking his way through tight spots. A smirk here, a laugh that rang a little too bright, and a stray fact about a missing hydraulic lift carried him through three sets of guards. He craved nothing more than to step through the last gate, and when he did, a wave of pride and terror crashed against him. Freedom tasted spicy, but he could still feel the kettle simmering behind him.

The city folded him into its moving heart: taxis spitting steam, market songs thrumming, a toddler looping a bright-red yo-yo. He slipped into the crowd like a drop of water on a fresh paint stroke. A hundred strangers jostled and bumped, but he sensed each of their faces weighing scales: the right slip and the neon badge would sparkle. He bit his cheek to stop the nervous flip of his eyes. The skyline glowed far ahead, a stack of bright promises. He pushed farther away from the UN roof, heart thudding out its tattoo, while he dreamed of the plane's rumble way up in the blue. The sun peeled away, painting the roads in caramel. Kofi slowed at the stop where the cement met the river and the world, for one long heartbeat, stood still. It felt like the quiet before a drum roll. Every street and alley leaned in, waiting for him to speak the next word.

Kofi could feel the line drawn behind him, and his crossing of it whispered only one truth: he could never go back. The weight of his decision pressed down on him like iron, but he pressed forward, every breath a promise to himself. He fought against the dark promise of the hunters on his tail, a storm he could never drown, and every pulse of his heart thudded the measure of his small, fragile freedom.

In a cell of twilight, Nova's eyes roamed the rows of pulsing screens, each one a hidden window into someone else's secrets. The glow painted her face opal, but the light could not mask the steadiness behind her gaze. Chief of covert analysis, her life was questioned and the quietly explosive answers that followed. The last seventy-two hours, a metallic rattle of alarms, warned that something deeper than customary treachery was afloat. Gathering signal curls and ghost echoes of conversations, she wove timelines like a tapestry, the colours of each player shimmering until they suddenly darkened. The web was real, and each careful fingerprint she placed against the wires advised her that the heart at its centre beat dangerously fast.

Someone was hiding in the dark and pulling threads, weaving a crisis meant to rip the power balance to shreds. Nova wiped sweat from her brow, her mind racing with the tangled threads of what was really happening. She knew the clock was counting down, but rushing ahead could spark an explosion they might never recover from. So she made herself steady, combing through the data with bulldog focus, hunting the one fact that could flip the script on reality. Her gut said the answer was buried somewhere strange, and she promised herself she would dig until she found it.

Days folded into nights as Nova waded through terabytes, drowning in numbers and graphs. She knew the tiniest detail could be a live wire, the smallest glitch a voice yelling, "Look here!" When the same strange signature popped up again and again across different roofs and grids, a cold fire shot up her spine. She could feel it—this was the break, the truth that could shatter all the comfortable lies.

Nova wove her thoughts into a clear, ruthless memo and shot it up the wire straight to the Command Council. The words struck like a siren. Conversations snapped to life, doors slammed, and the ancient, creaking machine of authority roared into motion. She did not stop watching until the first fleet of drones broke the skyline, and she felt an odd twist of hope and fear.

When the machine of power rumbled alive, Nova steadied herself for the shockwave that always followed change. The chessboard had been flipped, and now the pieces were hurtling into a confrontation on ground that changed by the hour, where loyalty had grown thin as smoke. Watching the world wobble on the edge of disorder, Nova realised she had launched a chain reaction her forecasts had warned about, a chain that would carve the path for whole nations.

In a chamber adorned with the scars of centuries of concession rather than for comfort, the delegates filtered in, each badge and whisper a testament to months and years of silent negotiations. Tension hung in the air, a palpable force, too thin to see yet too thick to ignore. When the Secretary-General raised his voice, the gravity of the situation seemed to intensify. Nova's eyes caught the subtle betrayals: a diplomat shifted in their seat, an ambassador avoided a third-hand compliment, a minister's hands clenched and unclenched.

The agenda, shrouded in half-light, was an outline of treaties, troop movements, and whispered creeds. Each spoken word, polished yet fragile, felt more like a rib than a word, threatening to shatter and reverberate down the jewelled corridors where maps were sleepless.

Elena stood behind a battered stone column, her gaze sweeping the chamber with the sharpness of a watchful cat. She noted every furtive nod, each accidental brush of a sleeve, and the hush that fell whenever a leader turned away. She knew the old map of pledges and betrayals by heart, and now, as the long arguments rolled on, she could feel the knots of old grudges tightening again. The talk of peace, of trade and of friendship was a beautiful thread, but one sharp pull, and it could snap, spilling knots everywhere. In the hush that hung between speeches, she sensed the moment slowing, as if the future hesitated to reveal its hand.

As the debate crested toward its greatest wager, a charged stillness hummed, and the dancers of decision hesitated, feet lifted. A sudden hush—barely a beam of light—cut through the thrum, and Elena's breath quickened. Omar appeared, gliding toward the lectern with the silence of falling snow. His face was a mask—no triumph, no fear—but something unguarded glinted in his gaze. He was a stone dropped in still water, and the ripples reached Elena, stirring buried doubts in every corner of the hall. The polite smiles wavered; behind them, old swords slid from their scabbards.

A quiet moment tipped the whole world toward change.

The whispers grew louder, and Elena felt the heavy secret, a revelation that could alter the course of history, hovering over her like a storm. She steadied her shoulders, knowing the wave about to break here would crash into every corner of the planet, well past the polished hall of the United Nations.

The room remained quiet except for the whir of the air conditioning and the tick-tick-tick of distant keys. Omar leaned over his screen, eyes glued to the glow while he combed through oceans of numbers and words. His hands danced over the keyboard, slipping through fortified files, pulling loose threads of the fabric that, if felt, would send high towers toppling. Each burst of symbols on the terminal hinted at the crooked truth that cloaked the strongest powers on Earth. Hours bled into nights, and nights gave way to more nights while the data streamed on, his brain crackling with the quake he felt coming. The dump was surgery, every byte yanked free on purpose, every secret laid bare to the light. The more he sorted the flakes into form, the more ice settled inside, because he carried the truth that could fracture the globe's very frame. Anger and will wrestled inside him every time he hit a lock meant to stop him, every time guards and ghosts popped up to wrestle the keys from his hands.

The firewalls and the encryption bounced pound for pound against Omar, yet he would not back down. He locked onto the task and used every programme, every exploit, every ounce of barely-legal firepower he had learned, until the ingenious barriers cracked. It became a chess match of milliseconds, his mind sparking against layers of silicon guardrails and mirror maze defences. Then, in the moment of silent fuse, every pixel on the monitor trembled and folded into a row of prototypes and chatter sealed in secrecy and scarlet. He leaned closer, and the chill of the impossible discovery washed over his neck. Here lay a redraft of the future itself, the kind they had warned him only ghosts of the old order could summon. The weight of this discovery, the danger it posed, was a heavy burden on his shoulders.

Inside the flood of code and couriers, lines snaked and lit up; a proton pathway of assassinated witnesses, coast-guard documents, mock condolences drafted at midnight. The threads the analysts had tossed away in earlier briefings now forged a single chart, furious and irrefutable. This was not a rumour; this was the bullet for the bulletins, the laser the cameras could not blur, everything needed to strip the pearl-coloured veil off the so-called alliance. Wet-eyed diplomats and half-remembered treaties of friendship were about to upturn into spectres of perfidy.

Omar's fingers over the keys trembled, not with adrenaline, but with the dread knowledge of what action now became unavoidable. Each second leaned heavier on the clock. He could send this fire across a thousand screens in a heartbeat, and the deafening truth would explode like the dangerous, uncontrollable wave he had sworn to ride. The urgency of the situation was palpable; every second ticking by added to the tension in the room.

He could almost hear the clock's ticktock growing louder in his own head. The secrets he cradled were explosive, and for every second they sat hidden, their power faded. Omar squared his shoulders and geared up for the next move, fully aware that every step was tangled with danger and hard choices.

Rumours of Omar's leak crackled across the globe faster than any firewall. Television screens lit up with blood-red accents; cable panels roared with speculation, staking reckless claims and repackaging unanswered questions as truth. Outside the United Nations, a throng of reporters charged the gates, blinking lenses and tongues on fire, and long-shelved documents spilt like rusty secrets. The crowd on the street, stacked up on tablets and half-bricked in their meat space jaws, inhaled every nugget as if it were the spicy kick of street food. Opponents in every capital filed impeachment motions and press releases, dancing on the vault of distrust, each clause a knife for the institution's already torched wings. In the eye of that bleeding cyclone stood Kofi, each gesture minutely amplified and rewired, every cleared throat reinterpreted as confession. Rumours of backroom deals and silent payments roared until they drowned out even the bored echoes of bureaucracy. On the cutting edge of that racket, shadowed hands scribbled new lines of the story, spinning triggers for the next act in a play that had never been meant for daylight.

The air hummed with a crackling hush while the whole world leaned forward, breath held, waiting for a truth, then waiting for each truth the world had a right to know.

The Outline spiralled and twisted like a double helix, a beautiful yet dangerous puzzle depending on the right piece falling exactly into the right place. Gathered in a half-lighted chamber where every shadow seemed to listen, the crew felt the weight in their chests like the first rumble of a storm. No one spoke the word failure out loud, yet everyone heard it. Nova, small and quiet under a silver shock of hair, mapped invisible tunnels of ones and zeroes, persuading the air itself to let her slip inside enemy networks and flip their signals like silent coins.

Across the table, Lena Petrov—whose blue eyes missed nothing—laid out scraps of hush-to-hush gossip, leaked dinners, whispered compromises she had stitched into a living diagram of who would sell a vote and who would buy a conscience at the UN. The clock above them counted in red, but the red was a flame. Omar, steady as the last star before the dawn, sketched their moving picture on the chalkboard—circuit, breach, exploit—his voice the first cup of black coffee every soldier drinks. They had dug bare wires in the statute books, run magnetic fingers along the soft underbelly of the blue helmets, and now only the last mile lay unmarked before them.

Kofi, the team's eyes on the ground, had prowled the UN's labyrinth until he knew the building's pulse—every guarded door, every forgotten fire escape stitched into his mind like a map of veins. With scanners humming in the gloom and only the creak of his boots for company, he'd marked out routes, blind spots, and shuttered lifts, until his dark ink sketches had become the threads of the operation. When talk turned to the halls themselves—long and echoing under a skylight cage—everyone nodded; only Kofi knew where the shadows thinned, and he would walk through them, not a whisper. The success of The Plan turned on his quiet certainty, underscoring the significance of his role in the mission.

Timing was a metronome ticking in the veins; the operation would live or die within a heartbeat. Outer cameras cycled on the minute, alarm loops and floors of ambassadors had their own tempo, and Kofi had choreographed the pulse. Elena, the team's wisp of smoke and broken glass, would be his twin; at the heartbeat's thinnest moment, she would ghost through the marble lobby, slip the guard's eye, and in the hush of the eighth tiger-striped corridor, lift the tiered intel locked in the UN vault.

As red laser grids and motion triggers shimmered on their holo-disks, the small room throbbed with quiet fire. The scent of burnt coffee and long nights hung in the air, but every shoulder clenched, every eye stayed bright. Plans were theories—this space was filled with the weight of embassies, borders, maybe the tilt of tomorrow. They lived inside the single certainty they had: they would not drop the thread. The room throbbed with a vow stronger than fear.

With grit in their veins and ironclad resolve, the squad

readied themselves to launch Operation Blue Star, aware that one squeeze of the steel trigger would twist the story of the world down an entirely new lane.

When the new, all-black phone buzzed on Kofi's desk at ten past midnight, a cold wind swept through the office. No name appeared on the screen, only a flashing, foreign set of digits, yet some deep instinct urged him to answer. He set his jaw, inhaled, and lifted the receiver—the chill of the plastic shocked him awake. The voice that spilt from the tiny speaker was a growl of cobalt static, layered beneath a calm that smelled of wires and midnight.

"Mr. Akins, we know the name you signed. We know the lab rabbit you bet on." The chill melted into ice. "But all of it can vanish if you honour our list."

Kofi's pulse thundered as the list unfolded, syllables tight as cuffs around his wrists. Images of the lab, of courses, and of the kids the courses had already swept up flooded him. He stood, layered on the knife edge, principles in one pocket, their faces in the other. The choice's shadow already stretched into tomorrow.

Kofi's spine straightened when he finally signalled with a stiff nod, and the decision sank around him like a rotten fog. When the call went silent, a buzz of alarm gnawed at him—seconds, not minutes, mattered now. He could already picture the spirals of the next hour and the hour after that, and he understood that he had just loosed the small, decisive pebble that would smash the glass face of the world's skyline. Bracing himself, he squared his shoulders and resolved to meet the night like a shield rather than the husk of a man, no matter the price. He would later discover that his choice, small in the hush of the moment, would yank the thread that teased apart the hidden stench in the marble halls, revealing rot that trembled beneath every treaty and flag.

The hush weighed like damp wool in the low room while Kofi measured the choice. Save the countless, and rivers of fire might yet dry; fire the fail-proof plan, and who knew which mirrors would shatter and fly. His fingers quaked just above the cool face of the hardened slate, breath slow and deliberate, heart loud enough to drown the quiet.

Outside, the city buzzed along, its people laughing and hurrying, blissfully ignorant of the storm that was already counting raindrops and building wind. Kofi could feel the countdown in every restless heartbeat; he had days, maybe hours, to correct a balance already tipped too far. The small box in his pocket hid a truth so toxic that to speak it would burn every hand that passed it up the ladder of lies. But the question hammered inside him like a burst drum: would the truth burn his own people too? His gaze flicked to the storefront photos of his mother and sister, beams of a happier time, and the image twisted. During lunch, his friends had joked about a faster server, their faces open and trusting, blissfully ignorant that his silence fed the poison. If he moved, their names would fill the casualty lists. If he stayed, the lists would fill anyway—only the children's names would anchor them. The scales tipped to the children.

Kofi's hand, shaking more from the weight of the choice than the chill of the room, pulled the switch. When the green light flicked on, dread slithered up his spine like smoke, but beside it a thin ribbon of light flickered—hope. The message launched on silent wings, a thread of pixels that might weave a new tomorrow or snap and wrap around their throats. His breath matched the hummed heartbeat of the device: steady, steady, steady. Kofi pressed his palm flat to the cold metal, feeling metres of distance and danger already. No road led backwards.

The die was cast, and all that remained was faith that his price would mean something. He let out a weary breath, steeling himself for the impending tempest, and understood that, win or lose, tomorrow's story would mark Kofi's daring as the hinge on which the future swung.

Chapter Three

THE FINANCIAL FUSE

Kofi walks the streets of Paris, blending in like any other local. This mission is critical. As the city's glow lit the streets, Kofi stayed on the move. Focused on the task at hand, he knew that he had the potential to lose everything he worked for. Kofi's determination was palpable for the first time, even as he mapped a way through the streets that had so confidently deemed the alleys a maze. Paris was Paris for a reason. It was a responsibility for a reason, but in this case, he could afford no mistakes. He could not even for a second believe that the person walking next to him was not a spy. Kofi's breath was steady, but he could hear in his ears the drumming of the city as though it were in sync with the second hand of the oh so precious clock.

The city's streets did not set the mood; the flickering of lights did, and as he readied himself to lose a record-breaking amount of time to history, Paris gave him a smile more comforting than he could have imagined. Its comforting smile was inviting him even deeper. The feeling was majestic, but Kofi was not there for a holiday. Watching time trickle through his fingers, coming in tedious and blurring minutes, was no excuse to let his mind wander. Paris was the city of love, but for him, today was not. He could not afford to miss even a microsecond.

The blaring sirens in the distance sent shivers down his spine, especially in the world he lived in. Kofi was making progress towards his target. The world was still shrouded in darkness, but a sliver of light was breaking through, and the dawn was just around the corner. In a split moment, Kofi was at the place he had been gearing towards. The building was enormous, and the sight of it was stunning, yet intimidating at the same time. Kofi was to take the first step towards making history.

His first step was not without its challenges. Kofi received a secret passcode, which led to vast amounts of digital currency, and it was time-bound. The only challenge was that he was bound to a time frame.

Kofi and his crew were in an endless storm of panic, trying to trace the origin of the financial catastrophe. As Kofi and his crew attempted to figure out the underlying cause of the looming financial apocalypse, Kofi sat and brainstormed code after code for solutions, straining his creativity to its limits. Kofi and his team were trying everything to ease the looming panic and financial meltdown of the company. With how offshore accounts and virtual money laundering were clouding the entire issue, their efforts were not yielding any results. The relentless urgency to crack the code pulled them into parts of the dark web that were crawling with danger. Kofi always believed in the quote that failure was not an option, and from everything that he was trying, it was not the best of options. As he was being pulled into more and more danger, Kofi was in for a digital ride, with every step coming with vengeance. All the suspense that surrounded Kofi kept dragging him into a virtual chase, with every step simulating a treacherous chess game.

Kofi needed their backup to hold the line, but their system was being riddled with endless code combination-dependent traps. Virtually the entire team was in a line, and one side was typing. The other was barely managing to navigate with constant hopping from button to button. Everything was coming crashing down, and the only conclusion that he was working to bring into fruition was a more sophisticated algorithm. Kofi hoped that each step he took would not turn out to be his mansion of errors, leading to his downfall. Somehow, with a sprinkle of luck, Kofi managed to crack the code, but not without a moment of panic.

Between the streams of electronic signals and the coded messages, they could sense a breakthrough coming. As Kofi and the others had imagined, a new lead pointed to someone compelling, hiding behind the curtains of the cyber world and controlling the financial fuse poised to set off global destabilisation. Right now, Kofi's icy nerves and a mind full of ideas were all that was needed to decipher the screenshots' metadata. The virtual battle was coming to a head, and victory was within reach, but the sovereignty of entire nations was at stake.

Elena's slender figure blended nicely with the personnel in the streets of Moscow, as she moved to the rhythm of a dance, looking at every angle to solve the new problem of the day that had been put in front of her. Making the appearance of a normal passerby, Elena felt as though she was suspended in the middle of a very finely woven web, with no way to turn back. At every step, she risked falling off a delicate tightrope.

She filled her description by default; her mission was to create a diversion which would be picked up by the cyber-security systems of the financial headquarters, while at the same time doing the exact opposite of directing scanners to centre her focus on the central systems of the headquarters. Elena had perfectly disguised herself as an executive with urgent business at the bank. She had mastered the rush like every professional anticipatory move; Elena was in control of the order. Her heartbeat was in sync with the chaotic rush that was about to be set in motion. Moreover, she had meticulously planned her distractions, which needed to be executed as set events that would prevent the focus from the changes taking place behind the closed doors. Elena had executed the first stage of the plan with a subtle motion as she began to engage the checkpoint guard with a question. In a few moments, without shifting her gaze, he was disengaged from work as he had a self-mesmerised gaze focused on the global economic trends. As if the doors had magically opened, her crew was already set to get in motion. Omar, the tech guru, had complete control of the data centre and was smoothly gliding as he entered the designated systems with keystrokes. He was doing the cautious yet speedy work. The timer was enabled, and he had no chances of errors.

Outside, Elena kept up her part of the distraction, skilfully pulling the guard's attention toward her with little hand movements and the right words at the right time. What she did not know was that two sharp eyes rested on her every move from the nearby rooftop. Perched on a rooftop, the sniper known as Kofi was watching and ready to act if necessary. The invisible danger that tailed Kofi made the work more nerve-wracking than it already was, revealing the constant threats, pulsating danger, and extra burden. Elena, however, did not give up. Drawing from her training, instincts, and intuition, she manoeuvred through the layers of deception with ease. The pressure kept mounting, and the atmosphere was pulsating with danger. An unforeseen twist was the last thing she needed, and that is precisely what Elena was trying to avoid. Innovating currently and with the right attitude, every domino that was set up to fall in Elena's path was dismantled ounce by ounce. Any unyielding resistance was a towering structure that mounted on her will in a compounded form to the risky moves she was ready and committed to undertake.

With all the confusion going on, one truth stood out: Elena's stunning performance had created a turning point for the climax, a shift between the forces of evil and the bold defenders of justice. Elena's actions were far more consequential than simply winning a battle: they sparked a series of events with far-reaching effects on the world's political scene. Between the shining skyscrapers and the hustle and bustle of the street, Elena's act of bravery had won epic and decisive battles, carved pathways to victory. It established a legacy of valour and victory for the ages in the hidden chronicles of history.

Omar's fingers worked like magic over the keyboard, bringing life into the soft glow of screens that dotted the space. Lines and patterns of numeric symbols formed financial webs that sparked intricate stories, and low, humming staples of the electronic world boxed Omar in. Tunnel-like, his multitiered world, encompassed with glowing screen partitions, a wizard like Omar, the digital world brought to life. Having spent years cultivating an array of sources and sensitive data on the world's most secure servers, an information broker and master of hacking, Omar always pored over the newest challenge.

He was a mysterious person who was thought to be the most sought-after individual in a clandestine world. In the smoke-filled room, he was a maestro conducting a symphony of cyber thievery. With skill unmatched, he was capable of full-scale digital war on sophisticated computer networks that lethally guarded national secrets. His fingers danced over the keys to a classified financial system, bypassing firewalls and encryption protocols. The data was at his mercy and came pouring in, uncovering complex and hidden webs of suppressed power and money that spanned the globe. Each data point added to the already complex map of multi-layered warfare between nations, companies, politics, and disguised alliances. Each second, he was silently gripping more and more of the tightly held secrets of the multi-trillion dollar business world, and digitally exposing countless of the most powerful people in the world. But how he wished he could go for a long, calm walk; the more he tried to focus, the more illusions he added to his digital maze. Some people, his instincts told him, were bounding in the shadows, ready to attack if he unwittingly crossed the lines of their carefully crafted plans.

Even though there was a chance that forbidden information could cause problems, there was also a chance that Omar could find the truth and gain leverage. Omar had an insatiable appetite for the inner workings of the world's economic power structures. As he was carving through the information, a tiny yet alarming idea began to register at the back of his mind. A slight lead was suggesting that there was a more profound and bigger riddle waiting to be solved. To Omar, it was a sudden epiphany. Amidst the multitude of authentic financial activities, there was a barely discernible anomaly that was telling the world there was more to behold. Equipped with newfound conviction, he began to pursue the path of the lead, combining instincts, technical skills, and luck. The more aggressive he got, the more entangled Omar became with a complex mesh of lies, bunco, and information. The more power and authority he was able to uncover, the more distinct and alarming the reach of his findings became. As a result, he was able to find the propelling factors of an unmarked clash of unmasked treasuries.

Kofi sat opposite the operative, her icy eyes fixed on him. In the softly lit room, silence enveloped everything. The murmuring of electrical surveillance gadgets broke the quiet. Kofi understood the need of the hour. Time was short, and answers were needed. As the silence threatened to stretch out indefinitely, Kofi lurched forward to start the interrogation. As expected, the operative was silent, refusing to give anything away. In silence, tactical close-quarter psychological warfare of interrogation began, word by word, posture by posture, the tight jaws and stoicism cracking step by step. The psychological grappling shifted and wrangled between him and the operative as the clock's hands unfolded cruelly, ticking down in Kofi's favour. Hours passed, and finally, the operative displayed some form of emotion. To prepare for the next offensive and let out some secrets, and in the process let some carefully constructed truths slip. Bolstered by fresh confidence, Kofi scrambled to the centre, peeling back the recently epoxied layers of mystery. As he focused on the operative, Kofi read her gestures, faces, and body language for hints of weakness or elaborate lies. Eyes sharpened, the quiet breathing in the room became suffocating as answers, hesitation, and emotions poured in, all the while Kofi inched closer and closer to the callous truth.

Then one day, the moment the operative's determination broke, everything they had stashed away was suddenly accessible. The concealed truths exposed revealed a state of secret operations within and outside the country. Kofi, at this moment, was sure that these pieces of intelligence were indeed the igniter, the moment everything was going to change. Those pieces of intelligence gathered exposed the cryptic view of the whole situation and the truths under the surface. Kofi felt satisfied and was able to suddenly stand while feeling directly motivated to advance the mission, fuelled by the pieces of information he had just uncovered. The results achieved by the interrogation were somehow better than he had expected. They only revealed the surface of an exposé of layers that covered the danger of the web of intelligence, secrets and treachery.

Kofi stretched out in the old swivel chair, letting his eyes drift to the ceiling like clouds searching for a place to rain. The week had worn him down, physically and soul-deep. He had always known the work carried a blade's edge, but he had not prepared for the cut to come from his own side. The team he would have sworn his life for had turned the spotlight on him, and the light burned like hot metal. Memory after memory poured into his mind, each like a grain in a roaring engine. Betrayal's cold hand and gnawing guilt squeezed his chest, yet under the storm, something inside him hardened like tempered steel. The truth had a heartbeat, and Kofi would track it down. He leaned in and let the pieces click and grind; a puzzle he had stared at for days suddenly whispered. A grain of dirt on a boot, a slip of a name in the break room, the wrong date on a report—small ghosts that now glared like prison bars. His voice, calm yet heavy, brushed the room's cool shadows. I will undress the lie thread by thread, every truth a knot that Jericho's walls cannot hide behind.

He understood that the betrayal went far beyond doubt; it revealed a wicked design that threatened everything. Gripping the last candle of hope that flickered inside him, Kofi vowed to snatch victory from the jaws of despair, to unmask those who wanted to snuff out the flame of his people, and to lay their dark plan bare before the world. Every injustice against him and everything he had sworn to protect must be made right. He stepped onto a path lined with peril and doubt, yet within his heart burned an untamed spark, fierce and unyielding, urging him forward to snatch justice and exact the reckoning he owed.

The silence of the dim briefing room held Kofi's voice like glass, unbroken and charged. Outside their walls, pressure was swelling like thunder, and the agency's heartbeat quickened. The instant of choice had arrived. Eyes lit with urgency, the squad members scrutinised the dark echo of their equipment, triple-checking, re-checking, memorising each snare whose most minor slip could snatch them into the void. Under the flickering stars, the team flowed like smoke toward the razor-edged compound, silent against the night and slipping through the enemy's gaze as a whisper of wind.

Their movements were sharp and steady, honed by months of disciplined training that had led them to this very night. The bulk of the compound loomed ahead, growing larger with every measured stride, the air thick with quiet anticipation. Once they reached the perimeter, the unit split into shadowy arcs, each member slipping into the cover that had been rehearsed until it felt like breathing. Elena, the team's ghost, guided them with laser focus, her quiet insistence steadying every jittery nerve. She slipped past the outer wall like smoke, silence swallowing her. The others melted in behind, already oriented toward the compound's darkened centre.   Inside the cavern of concrete and steel, Omar moved at a different front. Light screens from shelves of routers glowed in a hidden, blood-red laboratory. His hands danced, tracing a stolen cycle of code that unlocked gates and cameras ahead of them, pixel by pixel, heartbeat by heartbeat. They felt his calm through the earpieces, a heartbeat measured by circuit noise and clatter. They were together, miles apart. The breach led them deeper. The hum of fluorescent tubes became a tension string pulled taut. A slip or a flash could rip their cover apart. Every footfall that rang in the corridor made them swallow the urge to breathe. They moved like ghosts within ghosts, a mesh of nerves and night, drawn toward the centre that had once been a point on a map, now a heartbeat they had sworn to stop.

Suddenly, the quiet exploded into shrieking alarms. Regs' heart jumped. They had been spotted. He snapped the mic.
"Always nice to be invited to the party, huh?" and the team was off.
Order snapped back into place—fire, cover, movement—like practice drills on repeat. Bullets zipped and smoke bloomed, a storm of heartbeats and gunfire, and every second they fought harder to stay ahead of the mounting red dots on their screens. Out of the blast chorus, a distant voice hissed the grim news: reinforcements en route, and they had minutes, not hours. Regs could feel his bones respond—determination curling into every aching joint. They pressed deeper, facing not just enemies but a flood of bodies, shouting and shooting, one after another.
When the last charge of rifle fire cut off, the silence that followed almost hurt. They stood on a sea of blackened earth, the smoke curling upward like hands pleading for the past. The mission was a hard-won stamp; they had the data, they had the way out, but every wound on their skin felt like a contract they could not yet sign. The cost was inscribed in the faces beside them, the smell of burnt earth, and the distant

rumble of what would come next. Regs wiped the sweat off his brow, and voicelines buzzed like angry wasps: the real mission had just begun.

Patrick and the team tightened the last bits of gear, nerves humming like live wires.

The moment they got wind of the breach, they moved like lightning, plotting how to turn the tide before the worst could hit. Inside the still, sealed war room buried in the tower, every specialist leaned in: coders who could crack glass, analysts who could spin every number. The air crackled like charged air before a storm, but Patrick stood quiet at the head, calm as winter water, and the calm flowed outward. One slip, and not just ledgers, but the pulse of global trust could go dark. He felt every heart in the room and measured the scale: the ripples of today could map every tomorrow. The fight was now, and they had to out-watch the watchers. Monitors glimmered, fans hummed, and Patrick charted their counter-stroke like a composer at supper. While the red lifts rolled upstairs as if the sky were still blue, he guided the brightest toward the fragile threads the intruder had brushed too hard. The first breach had whispered secrets: when it came, how it crawled. They turned the whispers into a heartbeat they could synchronise, so the next lunge could slide right into a steel trap. The clock overhead ticked louder than artillery, and the room rolled forward a single hard step at a time—scripts, firewalls, backups—everything a soldier and a saint had taught him to hold. At the same hour, Elena, bright as a polished edge, lost herself in the vault of high-stakes journalism.

She drilled deep into the tangled web of covert ties and came up with explosive facts that would shine a spotlight on the motives driving the approaching danger. Her unflagging search for the truth ignited a chain reaction that hammered through every vaulted room of power, setting the scene for a truth that might level the sky. Time after time, even when noise and panic brewed, Patrick's steady heart steadied hers, firming her promise to chase the truth, whatever the price.

At the same moment, Omar's sharp dive into the flowing streams of data laid bare a clever tower of lies the enemy was stacking on every continent. His breakdown spelt out how the enemy twisted facts and fake sparks to hide their real hands, and in that same breath, Omar showed where their defences sagged. Armed with that clarity, the squad locked the enemy's every move under glass, carefully baiting a counterstrike that would yank the battle into the daylight.

As the countdown tightened, Patrick was shoved into a stark room with the enemy's chief enabler. Bones rigid, he leaned into the chair and shot question after question. With each answer dragged into the light, the enemy's shining veneer sliced apart, revealing the rust and poison between each gleaming promise. Justice burned in Patrick's core, but the clock also throbbed in his ears, shaping each question, each threat, into a gamble where the next heartbeat might either save a city or seal its fate.

Still, when the world around him felt like a tightening fist, he stood unbowed, his heart locked against the panic. At first, each tiny victory felt fragile, yet they snowballed, tightening into a single unstoppable gear. The leak, a carefully timed burst of truth meant to pierce the hidden machine, ricocheted through every trading floor. Lies that had drifted for years surfaced gasping, and the tremor shook governments, banks, and every pocket that had mistaken silence for safety. When the last echo faded, Patrick and his crew exhaled together, knowing they had beaten a titan without firing a single shot and that their names would ride the train of every future whisper about courage and cunning.

Midnight rang through the hushed city, and the towers crouched under a hush as thick as old money. Elena knelt behind frosted glass, the city a faint silhouette beneath her. Orbiting satellites danced like guardian fireflies, and she traced their paths with her gaze. Tonight, they would carry the truth. The dull screen before her lit her face a ghostly blue, and the countdown flickered in her chest, steady and cold. One last keystroke and the world would unwind in trembling pixels.

Across several continents, Omar wiped sweat from his brow and plunged deeper into the steel-cool aisles of the data centre. His fingers flew over the plastic keys, crafting a river of code so fine it felt like breathing on a blade. Nations lay like dominoes, each flick of his wrist stacking them into the dark. Meanwhile, Kofi, stationed in a small backroom lit only by his tall screen, wrestled with the night's final puzzle: a conversation locked behind a hundred-digit cypher. With every heartbeat, the window narrowed, and he hurled every resource he had against the firewall, trying to yank the truth into the open. Somewhere far above both of them, unseen hands spun a counterweb, watching every keystroke through holes only drones had holes for. In the gilded hallways of power, the word "disclosure" slipped from mouth to ear like a lit match through dry straw, and the same word quilted allies and enemies into a single threatening storm.

Then—the siren. A single, piercing note cut the night into fragments. The alarm roared truth aloud, unravelling the silk-threaded veil and sending it into digital wind. Screens flickered, and the Dow bent, then snapped, as the first slashes of proof cut out for every lonely analyst and every small trader beneath the same star. First shock, then avalanche: ledgers-zeroed, currencies-fled, and in dawn's cold light, the earth's cautious belly rolled over to face a new and terrible truth.

The giants of the financial world raced against the clock to seal the breach, but the doors of consequence had already swung wide. The fragile faith that had held the global economy on a wavering thread now hung in tatters, and the ripples of that breach promised to reshape entire corners of the future. The dawn that arrived, bathing the world in unwelcome amber and chill gold, brought with it a history now rewritten—each sunrise to follow would record the moment the world decided it had changed for good.

The leak unleashed a tsunami. Markets skidded, fragile pacts began to crack, and the public stared at institutions it had once respected with open mistrust. In the eye, Kofi, Elena, and Omar sat stunned, drawn into a tempest they had never seen forming. The consequences raced ahead of any compass. Their nations shifted into emergency laws, boardrooms shifted into war rooms, and the space between killings turned into a hunting ground. Kofi's crew became living equations whose answers scared the powerful. They dodged glow-lit pursuers, skimming the edges of empty overpasses and dark alleys, leaving only the fading pulse of sirens and the nameless wind behind them.

At the same moment, the world economy swayed like a tiny boat in a storm, rocked by the same lies that had just come to light. Every tick of the clock raised the stakes for Kofi and his crew, who were fighting the clock to expose the sabotage behind the upheaval. Pressure mounted and alliances flickered: some sparkled like good fortune, others snapped like dry twigs. Then came the hidden schemes and whispered motives that the light had never touched, and Kofi understood how big the storm really was. One wrong step and a human life might vanish, and every choice they made sent shock waves from Wall Street to small street markets. Together, they trekked through a shadowy maze where friends yesterday might be foes tomorrow, and even the truth wore a mask. The ordeal stripped them of comfort and rest, testing their courage and cunning until they were nearly frayed. One by one, they pulled loose threads, unravelling the evil that seemed ready to tear down the pillars of the world economy. Then silence fell. The old skyline still hummed, but a new wind was blowing. The puppeteers who once pulled strings now felt the blade of new powers they had ignored. The map of influence the old had drawn in ink had bled, and Kofi and his crew were left staring at the blurred edges, wondering how the world they saved—yet had changed—would treat them at sunrise.

After the storm passed, they stood together, staring across a horizon where everything shimmered like shattered glass. Each decision they'd made, each moment they'd hesitated, now whispered in ticketed voices the kind that never leave, the kind that writers study for a century, waiting for metaphors to grow around the wounds.

Chapter Four

The African Front

Lagos, 10:00 AM: Rising Tides of Conflict

Cool morning air skimmed through Lagos, threading unease under every footstep. Distant thunder rumbled somewhere above the street vendors, while the sun poured gold onto rooftops and wires like molten metal. From the rooftop of a dull tower, Kofi watched the million rooftops, the moving crowds, the sigh of the harbour, and the illusion of calm masquerading as a dawn. The wind felt like the edge of a blade. In a cramped, bright-walled room lit by whispered screens and scattered files, Kofi sat bent over a flickering console. His years had taught him to read the city like a map that redrew itself each hour. Around him, faces grown tight by purpose translated the latest fragments of nervous chatter and flickering satellite blips into meaning. Line by line, the wires whispered warnings, and image by image, the screens laid bare the circuitry of ruin: ordinary-looking citizens, balanced between bank queues and street prayers, exacting a slow betrayal. The diagram spreading before them glimmered like a net, and somewhere in that net lay the anchor for the coming night.

The team traded quick, sidelong looks, faces taut beneath the low light, knowing the news alone had changed everything. Croft, always just a whisper in the darkness, had pushed his hidden war deeper, planning a strike aimed straight at the lifelines that kept Africa steady. A wound like this would bleed outward, unspooling tensions fast enough to snare any nation in the storm. Kofi felt the moment for debate slip away; the only answer was to move, and move hard. Inside the war room, the quiet was thick with dread, broken only by the low, steady shrug of servers scouring mountains of code. O-minutes blink overhead, feeding in satellite shots that ironed the continent with fresh light, each red dot a mark on a resource the future of millions depended on. These arteries of power, road, water, and hope once seemed invulnerable, proof that yesterday's dreams could be tomorrow's reality. Croft's choice to sever them, from a desk many miles away, proved his war was one fought by snakes who struck at the weak. Kofi drank in the sight of each blinking red pin, remembering the weathered faces of the men and women who had crossed rivers of red earth to vote for this prosperity. Their stories of endurance, stitched into his DNA like scar tissue, knotted tight in his throat. That history would not allow him to turn away; it transformed duty into fire.

He didn't have the luxury to waver; the moment before him shimmered with unbearable keeping. Already the dark clouds of war crawled across the continent, and Kofi squared his shoulders to meet the storm, accepting the heavy, sacred duty meant to shield tomorrow's children.

The midday sun hammered Lagos, roughing the streets in a dry gold. Kofi flowed between stalls and taxis like water, loose laughter and the smell of yams and engine oil were his only armour. His eyes cut across the crowd, seeking the faint misalignment of a furtive glance. Years in the National Intelligence Agency had trained him to read the air for the whisper of a gun, the twitch of a lie. Today, though, it was the quiet hammering of his own heart that threatened to crack his calm. The telephone had shrilled in the dark hour, his mother's voice a thin line of chill that skated across the waking night: come home, come home; the village was watching the road, watching the distant fires, watching for him.

A shudder of dread washed over Kofi, a feeling that had crawled under his skin ever since the phone call. Duty and love twisted in him like a dagger and a bandage, both shouting for his loyalty. He had sworn an oath to guard his country, to stand the line without flinching. Yet, his mother's voice—small, shaky—broke like a kite string above the drum of gunfire in his mind. How could he leave her now, when the doctors had just whispered "two months"? But if he stepped away from the post, the front cracks would widen, and the predators circling the nation would gamble her safety for a fast kill. He kept pacing the blistered streets, the choice grinding inside like a shard of glass no rain could wash out. Ahead of him, the road was a dark maze, each footprint falling toward a new, sharp question. The creed of the soldier hummed in his bloodstream, the price of the star he wore, while his mother's hush of misery knotted tight in his throat. He pressed on, legs moving like stone, the ghost of family on one shoulder, the ghost of country on the other. Whatever he decided tonight would re-stitch the incomplete quilt of his life forever.

In the hush of the backroom, smoke coiling from a single lightbulb, Kofi's eyes locked on the crumpled map that lay like a bad confession on the table.

His fingers lingered over maps stained with routes and suspected flashpoints; the weight of his task pressed hard on his chest. Duty yelled from one shoulder, the soft cry of family from the other, and he sensed the old, familiar threads of his life beginning to fray. An old ache spread in his chest, the ghost of every past choice, and insisted on the one terrible fact: so many futures hung on his words. Inside the marble halls, the careful art of shaping stories had grown more powerful than treaties. It was no longer enough to lay facts on the table; one had to choreograph every glimmer of light and shadow. A whisper in the press, a pause in a speech, a tiny alteration of timelines—God help them, each tiny fit of air—could forge friendships or fracture nations. Kofi had learned such lessons. The nib of his pen floated over waiting paper, choosing, weighing lines that tomorrow would stand under the eyes of presidents, journalists, and millions who sensed only the heat of the fire and not its dance. The ghost of Meridian spread its wings over every choice, twisting trust into smoke. The riddle of the bitter rift demanded exposure, each knot undone so daylight might expose its colour. Yet, in a world of shadows and signals, the border between light and dark had become a thin and changing line, and Kofi walked its length armed only with ink, searching for a truth that would not betray him.

As night deepened, Kofi fought to turn the raw truth of the world into a story that would knit people together without losing honesty. Diplomacy felt like a slow, steady dance, balancing clear sight with the wisdom of keeping some cards close. Mistrust had already ripped the global quilt, and Kofi wanted to weave a new thread that would bring the torn pieces together. Then, caught in the maelstrom of treaties and talks, a sudden light flickered in his mind. The words he poured out would be more than ink and parchment; they would be the slender, shining walk across a dark gap, a little fire that would not flicker out even in the thick fog of doubt. Heart steady, he dipped the quill again, forging a story able to face Meridian's lurking shadows without bending. The chamber hush pressed in close, only the steady hush of quill on parchment filling the air, drawing truth's quiet lines through the thunder of lies.

The digital sphere sprawled like a dark, twisting maze, dotted with flickers of light. Every link, every heartbeat of code, guarded a country's secrets and a tomorrow's fortune.

Inside the quiet storm of circuits and light, Nova danced between duties of protector and silent saboteur, her fingers tracing code the way a pianist strokes a familiar sonata. She had slipped past a hundred shields and stood now in the marrow of Meridian, a monolith whose chill breath swept every ocean. Each novel loop she cracked thrust her deeper into a coverlet of lies wrought by the corporation's unseen hands. Alert and unyielding, she gathered the disjointed sparks and spun them into a pattern, reweaving the nightmare the enemy believed uncuttable. Yet, even in this war of zeros and ones, Nova felt a roar beneath the code, a rancour that soared beyond vaults and ledgers, past the simple urges of profit. Meridian's poisonous reach coiled around the marrow of life itself, bending breath and heartbeat for an unseen purpose. Track by track, she followed the path of blackmail and puppet strings, a lattice so tightly wound that waking and dreaming blurred. Each truth she seized drew her nearer to the shadow behind the crown, the unseen puppet master whose name had never left the hush.

The moment sown darkness tightened its grip around Nova, she understood at last. This war was no longer just a cyber skirmish, but a clash for the very heartbeat of human choice. With the last fragment of forbidden code burned into her mind, she slipped into Meridian's labyrinth for the last time, ready to fight the abstract nightmare that had danced beyond her reach for too long. Every ally might now be a spy, every signal might lie, but the weight of entire nations hovered above her, trembling. Nova pushed forward into the neon silence, pulse steady, knowing that what the darkness revealed at the core would redraw every frontier, perhaps carve the very sky under which every living soul would yet dare to hope.

The ocean wind slid between the palms like a ghost, bringing the taste of brine and the ache of a question. Standing at the quay of Lagos, under lanes of neon and diesel, Omar watched the amber sun kiss the waves and disappear, wave after wave swallowing the last light.

In moments like this, when silence hugged the air like a stretched hush, Omar felt peace while the world outside still shouted. He had set down the rifle long ago, but now carried a sharper armament: understanding. The evening deepened, the sky folded, and he slipped back into the hush of his little room, a canvas of fold-out tables and borrowed chairs. Overhead, the worn fluorescent tube flickered like a stray star, and its grey light stopped at the edges of his table, where rows of darkening screens waited. Each of those screens, like tired eyes, carried the dent of sleepless nights spent tracking the phantom trails left by agents who tugged at the world's thin sheen of safety. The night folded in like a curtain, and Omar leaned in ever closer, stitching continent to continent. He sorted rows of masked signals, a chessboard of glyphs, and every symbol he pried apart felt like a dent in the hush, leading him sideways, without light, to the hidden truth. Restless still, he let his hands fly across the keys, steady and hard, pulling at knots of light that tired, then gave way, spilling schemes too dark to name. Before the first grey of dawn, while the sky still hesitated, a shape flickered: a gentle, awful truth, drifting across the circuits like smoke but clearly marked by a living hand.

The glowing screen showed a pattern—cold, twisted, almost beautiful—made up of ones that moaned like ghosts. Each cluster was a signal sent by an enemy who knew every crack in every nation's armour and spent years weaving a net they thought no one would ever touch. For too long, these shadow-cutters had worn the darkness like a coat, whispering in hidden rooms, tracking every secret, lowering thin threads of doubt and ruin into the hearts of the unwary. Omar took a breath that steadied the tremor in his hands and pressed the next key, marking every knot in their invisible rope that bound powerful men through lies, every pivot that turned sorrow into rule. The fingerprint buried in strange, humming glyphs was the lantern that would burn the night flat, revealing the grey faces crouched behind twitching neon masks. Somewhere behind that blinking watcher, an architect was polishing the next tremor in the world's spine, and Omar stood between him and the dawn. Outside, the ordinary shapes of the city tasted the first heat of daylight, unaware that the storm crouched behind their screens. Omar slipped from the small, humming room, spine like steel, eyes lit with the fire of a promise the darkness would never keep.

What he had found felt like the first crack of thunder before a storm that could swallow the sky. He understood that chasing the truth from here on would drag him through a whirlwind of danger and hard choices. Yet, facing lies that cloaked everything, Omar rested his hope on one unbreakable fact: the human heart could bend, could bruise, but would never bow. As long as that inner flame burned, darkness could hurl anything it wished, and still, the light would not be snuffed.

When sunlight fell behind the jagged hills, the world turned to ink, and the team felt the chill of it crawl along their spines. Shadows stirred longer than they should, and the scent of dry soil mixed with the ghost of storms yet to come. Weeks of slow, gritty travel through red dust and stories half-spoken had come to this razor night. The target, a wisp of a name—"Meridian"—drifted through secure channels the way smoke drifts through wire. No photograph, no fingerprint, only a thrum of fear shared in muffled rooms where candles drown in wells of meaning. Forward motion now felt like sinking; every meter carried the weight of a fathomless dark.

Between gun attaché and battle-scarred medic, distrust crackled like the first stars. Luggage in the cargo hold carried old, aching ghosts: friends left behind in choke-lit alleys and rooftop graves. The mission promised a belt of justice, yet it wore the heaviest buckle—payback for every musty, silent hour spent studying prevention reports that had saved no one. They strapped night eyes onto fatigued round faces, shared half-words, and stared toward the void that promised answers only in rifle speed and resolve. The reckoning rode the wind, and only the wind answered back.

The land itself seemed to hold its breath as they crossed

the empty miles, the air big with silence except for the odd sound of animals waking and the thin beeping of their radios. Every step drew them farther into the night's own heart, and slowly, piece by piece, the calmness of the soul began to wear thin—inexorably tugged outward by the force of the hidden enemy. Yet within that anxious darkness, one fact kept its cool shine: they were the bait. Meridian, the patient stalker, had spun them into the night on purpose, twisting the fragile strings of politics and pride to pull them step by step toward the fatal crossing. The knowledge landed like a stone among them, a clear warning that the line between mission and the avoiding of death had grown too narrow to guess which was which. Still, under the load of that truth, a narrow, but steady flame of will kept the blood warm; it told them they would not come home empty. The team accepted the role of the lure without complaint, reshaping the shame of being hunted into the advantage of letting the hunter believe the field was all his. The darkness was still dark, but they were no longer afraid of it.

Their chase would draw them ever deeper into the winding passages of the labyrinth, to the place where night swallowed the last ember of light and Meridian crouched, veiled in smoke and riddles. Within the slow sweep of twilight's tide, they would stand above the yawning void and either overthrow it or be swallowed whole, the tremors of that moment ringing out across the bone-dry plains of Africa.

When the sun slipped below the western rim and the first stars dimmed the thick Lagos air, the skyline glowed like a poisoned bloom. Within that dying light, a thin, metallic stillness crept through the streets like smoke, summoning the operatives to a hushed rendezvous below the pulse of the city's skull. The meeting hung between smoke and silence, a tightrope of secrets and borrowed power, drawn tight across the new fractures that gouged the continent.

Candle flames fretted, and Kofi, the old commander with the map of scars across his knuckles, sketched the shadows now thick enough to bite. His voice rolled slow and heavy, almost an incantation; the urgency bowed the candles. They listened with the tautness of bowstrings: the ground was tilting, the by-laws of survival rewriting themselves with the crawl of night.

It wasn't just about reacting to fast-approaching danger; it was about rewriting the story of a continent that seemed ready to crack apart. When the plan began to breathe, a quiet fire filled the room, an unspoken promise to stand as shields against the gathering winds. We hammered out the blueprint, stitching secret pacts on threads of doubt. Every agent laid a piece of hard-earned skill on the table, knowing the only way to dodge the avalanche was to move as one. From the crowded streets of Lagos to the sun-baked arms of the Sahara, the clash refused to stay within neat maps. This was a fight beyond worn-out ideas, a war of half-seen shapes and half-heard voices drifting over desert and delta. The call to the continent rose like a piece of music, rich with fight yet tipping toward a future no one could name. We felt that stopping a land on fire called for a steady hand, a seeing beyond the veneers of rulers and armies. When the gathering finally stretched to a hush, the unbroken promise of every agent lingered in the smoke-slick room, a vow etched in the forges of the impossible.

The road ahead was only a black smear beneath the night sky, but the operatives moving down it kept a fierce, steady flame lit in their chests, a flame that turned the darkness into moving, manageable shadow.

The bleaching West African sun fell down upon the meeting like a hammer as delegates arrived at a hidden Lagos compound, each one sent by a nation still scarred from the last wars. No flag was present from any winner or any superpower. No one entered the compound by chance; they entered as soldiers of memory. Each delegate was a living dossier of alleys choked with fragments, open graves, and the daily price of living the hour. The responsibility pressed against their backs like the heat itself.   Inside the air-conditioned chamber, the ceiling hum was like distant thunder. Voices rose and fell, guarded and raw. The room still tasted of burnt ozone and burnt past. Here, the discussion became a different draft of air, one that tasted like smoke and communion. No single signature could dry the tears, but the delegates kept signing, the pen scratching out a new hymn. This was no list of articles; it was a living scar being threaded into a new skin. Each clause was a promise that the drought in one nation would not be treated as a border, that the cargo of one refugee would not be dropped like a stone. They were not just diplomats; they were knitters of a stretched, ordered, restless fabric, swearing that tomorrow's fires would be met with a shared bucket of water.

The arguments flew hot and loud, some rising to roars, others to wounds that would never quite heal. Yet, who could have imagined that from such fire would spring anything like light? Delegate by delegate, they began, slowly and stubbornly, to lay down the old grudges, sinking narrow ruins of the past into new, shared earth. When the city's red dusk spilt over the courtyards and palaces, they spoke the agreement, and it was no momentary peace. It was a vow, plain and binding, to meet every rising tide with backs pressed close together. It was forged not to win elections, but to win tomorrow.

Out on the streets of Lagos, the horns and laughter and haggling of ordinary lives never paused, never knew of the quiet thunder within the compound. Yet, within those ancient walls, every sentence spoken, every silence held, had already carried the first gasps of a different dawn. When the delegates stepped into the evening, the resolve on their brows was like storm-warning lanterns.

Their fellowship, hard-earned and still young, burned like a single, stubborn flame against the night that loomed beyond every window and every door. It stood, and still stands, as a loud no to despair and a quiet yes to every ounce of possibility still carried within a wounded but unbroken heart.

Across the pulse of Africa, a connection had crystallised, defying barriers, beliefs, and old wounds—an understanding stitched together by hardship and poised to steer the continent's tomorrow.

Elena's chase had carried her from continent to continent, her resolve a flame that would not gutter until the puzzle at her back cracked open. In the woven labyrinth of Lagos, she glided, step by step, calculated, her skin prickling at the burn of spice and exhaust that thickened the rainy air. Shapes stitched themselves at the edge of her vision, their flicker a reminder: she was never the only player in this calculated storm. The presence of hidden hunters urged her feet faster, so each wet alley turned into a fresh ambush and each idle face a possible sun-bright spy. Truth was her only currency, yet the scales of trust lay emptied. When the sun bled orange behind the horizon's towers, the city's breath shifted, and the heartbeat of the night adjusted. A pattern of footfalls rippled the murmur of horns and vendors, plain and fracture-like, and she knew the chase had grown a new leg—she was not alone.

Unshaken, Elena picked up her stride, head swirling with plans to lose the ghosts hunting her. A hurried glance over her shoulder showed only the dim, jagged shapes of giant towers, their shining skins dimmed by the creeping dark. Each heartbeat pulled her deeper toward the stillness where hidden truths lay coiling in the fog of the unspoken. The darkness pressed tighter with every footfall, yet her resolve sharpened, daring her to plunge farther inside. The hollow hush of the lonely alley sharpened her ears, urging her legs to quicken. A flash of bright metal sliced the night, a cruel star in the dark, and without thought, she ducked into the narrow hush of a doorway, bones drumming like fists against her hollow chest. Through the sliver of light, she scanned for a way to slip the still-hungry blackness. Here, in the city's underbelly, life balanced on the razor of instinct, skill, and an audacity that refused to blink. Summoning every taught reflex, Elena steadied her breath, reading the night behind her with the steadiness of a dialled-in rifle, sure that around the next bend of hush lay the distracted light she had to grab.

Dust and sweat drifted like ghosts, proof of endless grind by hands and steel.

Across the African plains, life and battle shared the same breath. Golden savanna stretched forever, but under the same sun, bones of long-fallen fighters glinted like cruel stars. Dust whipped past Kofi's boots, and he scanned the sky. Somewhere over the dunes, the enemy was waiting and preparing, the only proof a ripple of movement too distant and sun-blurred to confirm. Flies settled on the barrels of guns as the squad tightened belts and lips. Somewhere in the back of his mind, he could hear the drum roll of the oncoming fight. Kofi steadied his stance, forcing his hand to unclench the map that felt like iron on his palm. The burden of his rank was a heavy cloak, but he carried it without a tremor. Weeks of planning felt like a birth—not his alone, but of a strange, beautiful new nation born from many. Impartial old borders faded as men and women from the Atlas to the Zanzibar shore had marched up together, the old feuds packed away in sea chests. Generals and lieutenants blinked sweat from their eyes, drawing red circles on the sheet, daring the red to turn green and mean victory. Strategy was a prayer whispered in the flame's breath, and Kofi was the voice refusing to tremble.

The clang of final preparations was broken only by the

deep rumble of engines rolling across the hardpan; their growl anchored the moment and warned of the gamble. In the centre of the circuit of tents, a knot of field ghosts leaned close, their shadows riding the bright edges of the tents. Nova, a code-weaver whose hands moved faster than the fall of shadows, peeled apart layers of scrambled radio chatter. The message peeled away – a name less alive than smoke – a brotherhood that meant to nurse a continent to the brink of ruin. Omar, bent over a field chart, let his thin smile break only when a new line crackled under his fingertip, a fresh puzzle slid into the open where chaos might be forced to reveal its spine. Elena, a ghost of anything but operational memory, moved the wire-cutting world outside like a pacing ghost, eyes running over every rustle where most men would see only the night. When the sun folded its wings, the camp held its breath beneath the savage white of the lights and a few nervy stars. The hush did not hush; it hummed like a confident wire, promising early violence and only one end. The ground that would open tomorrow was not empty; it waited, already lined with the carved names and bone dust of all who had ever bought the ground a moment longer.

Far from the eyes of the globe, this lonely outpost quietly balanced the fates of entire nations on a thin thread, turning the everyday ground beneath its feet into a battlefield of secrets, where borders hardened and futures collided.

Chapter Five

The Lagos Gauntlet

Nova and Kofi stepped off the plane and into Lagos's furnace of an afternoon, the sticky heat wrapping around them like a wet sheet. The city pulsed with colour and noise, a carnival above ground and a quiet rumble below. Everybody was moving, bargaining, planning the next meal or the next big deal, and there in the crowd, Nova felt the government's hand was nowhere. The glittering glass towers shot straight up, too proud to tip their hats to the shanties clinging to their feet. She stopped, then stepped forward, the gap between them so wide it felt like a fence. Every floor of luxury above the tin and tarp below was a score, a barrel of gunpowder under a match.

They pushed through the streets, a living hurricane of voices and engine fumes. Bicycles and megabuses edged toward her like a wave, horns blaring the same two notes over and over like a stupid tune. In every narrow passage, the stalls burst sideways into the open, bright cloth, louder screams, and the humid perfume of red pepper, frying fish, and tired bodies. Kofi moved like moving water, feet sure, shoulders loose, a man in a river of men. His smile was a small slate-grey stone; it said, I'm here, but the rest of the city was not too sure. His eyes were two edge-lit lanterns, glancing the roof above him, the speed of the crowd, the pocket that might hold or heaven forbid not hold.

Nova couldn't help but appreciate Kofi's calmness, the easy way the street people tilted their heads toward him: part greeting, part caution, part respect. Their mission hinged on such comrades, folks who could map the invisible braids of trust and tension that wound through Lagos like the unseen currents of its river. Kofi had smiled and promised he could lead them to those who thrived between the streetlights, who whispered to the night and bent it to their will.

So it was that they found themselves an hour later in a place where the bulbs hung like lost teeth and the air hung thick like a dream. Hands lowered, voices lowered, everything weighted with the sound of small steel and smoky quiet. They slid like shadows to a corner table, where the smoke might hide them. There, the city offered its underbelly: men with teeth like yellowed pearls, women whose eyes ordered fortunes, both holding loyalties that changed with the turn of a card.

Nova and the others understood—each nod they returned was a promise and a warning. Every whispered pact was tied to a fine thread, and the wrong tug could unravel them all. There was more to Lagos than trade and currency; here, the measure was complicity and silence. They moved through the room as dancers on thin ice, never letting the heart of their purpose bob to the surface, for the river listened and the jaws beneath it were sharp.

In the swirling chaos of dusk, Nova and Kofi pressed on, certain that victory lived only in the loyalty of the right allies. When the city turned to burnished bronze and the last light of day fled, they already sensed the more challenging battles waiting in Lagos's shadowy streets and the secrets tucked in its narrowest lanes.

Fire danced in his blood as he pushed through the Lagos streets, the crowd a surging river of sound and colour. His heart hammered the beat of urgency, each stride a promise he could not break. The neighbourhood called him its hero; he wore the title like old cloth, rough but beloved, stitched with nights spent shielding the innocent and chasing shadows that mistook the city for its playground. Tonight, the game had tipped.

Wailing sirens stitched the air, and the city's pulse quickened. Though the street churned with life, his focus cut like a knife. Squinting past the street vendors, past the scrim of late light in the taxi's windows, his eyes searched for the telltale crack of danger. Each inhale tasted of heat and smoke; each exhale carved out a vow of defiance, sharpened by years of meeting storms at the door and not stepping aside.

They talked about him like he was a ghost that walks the streets in daylight, caution lacing their praise. The city had dressed him in the cloak of legend, a figure who turned the word "hope" into a living breath when all the lamps of trust guttered. Through the stillness of every midnight, when almost everyone was afraid, only he moved, quiet as a promise. Inside his ribs, however, the drum of responsibility never stopped. Each heartbeat reminded him that the lives of others dangled like lanterns on his every step.

The alleys twisted like secrets, painted with half-remembered fights and alleys that fed into alleys, and he strode through them as a needle through cloth. Every tiniest sound read like a page. Friends and informants, the brave and the broken, passed their watches to him: a broken watch, a half-lit street, a name whispered beneath breath. Together, they wove a net that caught evil lightning before it struck. Where darkness thickened like smoke, his watchful, unblinking lantern still cut a clean, straight line.

He kept moving, the light never wavering, because justice had no place to rest. Each threat he faced fed the city's rumour mill, turning ally into possible traitor with the speed of a knife. Still, the hero folded every ache, every doubt, into the armour of his heart and carried it like his own flag. Courage, he had learned, was the mirror in which everyone else recognised themselves.

With every second that passed, the mantle of heroism settled like lead on his back, a weight he lifted without a second thought for the people who hid behind his bulwark of courage. In Lagos, he was no mere mortal—he was a living myth, a flickering flame for a city hungry for a champion. Now, as the sun folded itself into the horizon, he felt the vow he'd made blazing brighter than the twilight, for he was the everyday marvel whose tale would outlive both clocks and stars.

The deeper he plunged into Lagos's hidden belly, the clearer the invisible city became—each alley and gutter illuminating a colossal, sinuous Network that coiled and recoiled on itself like smoke. It was not limited to gunmen counting the columns of their loss, nor was it rooted in crooked chairs in tainted boardrooms. Instead, it leaked into shops whose shelves gleamed, to politicians whose smiles never reached their eyes. Once he broke the ground, the proper soil revealed itself: something that thought and breathed without a body.

Nor was it anchored to bricks and blood. In the other Lagos, the one that flickered in the dark green of screens, another tribe was at work—ghosts of code, tin-hearted brokers, and murmurs that coin no coin. Here, a password was a rifle and a rumour was a gun. The horizon of Lagos was no longer a line: it was a mesh of consequences that rippled between the living and the zeroes that passed for life.

This underground world of code and smoke thrives on rumours, betrayals, and whispered promises of power. Moving with equal ease through cold alleys and glowing screens, our hero learns the lesson the hardest way: whoever controls the code and the concrete controls the future. Every footfall through the maze tightens the noose. The closer they get to the puppet-masters pulling the city's strings, the louder the clicks of unseen locks and the sharper the edges of unseen knives. Rogue eyes now track our hero through shifting tunnels of light and shadow. The Network has sensed the tremors of an intruder, and the dormant traps awaken, eager to taste the trespasser. Inside this world, every wish, every darker ambition coiled together like wires in a ticking bomb. One slip, one beam of careless light, and foes on every side will strike as one. In the merger of flesh and frequency, the stakes burn hotter: sheltering loved ones means walking the razor's edge. Spin the threads, break the threads, or be caught forever in the inescapable weave.

William pushed a chair to the centre of the bare room, the scraped metal sound swallowed by the hush. Candlelight guttered in a glass cup, and the shadows leapt like guilty secrets. He studied the man opposite, trying to pull the truth from the shifting light that skimmed across a face streaked with temporary pain and calculated calm.

Tension lay like fog in the dim room while he readied himself to pry loose the secret that might tip the mission. The prisoner stayed still, eyes locked on William like iron. Each tick of the clock stretched out, an invisible contest of endurance. At last, William shattered the quiet, tone calm but unyielding, and began peeling away the lies that cloaked their path. For an instant, the captive's mask slipped, a thin shimmer of doubt showing. William pressed on, steps measured, threading questions like scalpel edges, and the smallest gap in the man's armour widened. Bit by bit, the defence sagged, and the first, salty drops of truth began to flow. The room watched the fragments assemble, a dark design unfurling wider than they had feared. Hour by hour, William felt the balance tilt their way, strands of data tangling into a single, sharp story that lifted the curtain on the malevolent unseen. But just as the last shadow began to lift, a howl burst through the door, boots and barking voices ripping the calm. The sudden blast shattered the fragile gain, throwing doubt across the table and into their deepest hopes.

William wasted no time. He cuffed the captive tightly, then raced out into the storm. The city howled around him, every corner hiding a fresh trap, every shadow a potential traitor. He clutched the flashlight of the mission against the night's thudding heart. The bottom line hammered into him: the fight had just fired its first shot.

Electric tension rippled through the rooftop hideout as the squad stringently checked their gear. Surrounding them, Lagos had tightened its noose. One crack, and their figures would dissolve into memory. Drops of sweat trickled down their temples, but every pulse hammered, "go." Lung by lung, they inhaled the same dark air, eyes locked with purpose.

The moment the last sunbeam wilted, they exhaled the plan they had turned to muscle. No chatter wasted the magic: each had rehearsed their ghosts. They slipped into the city's veins, through twisting alleys and across bustling markets, shadow and passenger. Engines, shouting, horns merged into a thundering blanket. Under it, the team vanished out of sight, turning every footstep into a set of blank tyres.

Hearts pounding louder than drums, they skidded to a stop when the road ahead turned into a wall of armed men. The tick of the clock turned sticky, stretching every second. With no safe path behind them, they locked eyes and set the plan in motion. The flare of a flash bang and the roar of a hastily tossed smoke grenade painted the street in blinding colours. The gamble worked—guards turned, and the tiny gap that opened was just wide enough for them to dart through.

The city line ahead sparkled like a promise, but relief melted fast when sirens screamed in their ears. They were the hunted now, sprinting through alleys and narrow lanes like shadows. Desperation squared their shoulders, and rage turned every breath into fire. Sirens howled, tyres screeched behind them, but the team stayed glued to the one goal: finish what they'd started and keep the mission safe.

At the safe corner—a cracked wall with a blue door—breath caught in their chests, half fear, half hallelujah. They leaned, lungs heaving, and shared shaky smiles that felt like small suns in the night. The road had almost swallowed them, but somehow it had spat them back out. Bruised but not broken, they had tested their limits and, against all reason, lived to tell the tale.

They had held on so tightly to their purpose that they now found themselves on the edge of the future. The city was already shrinking behind them, the headlights turning streetlights into stars. Ahead was the road they had chosen and the curves they could not yet see. Every mile they put behind them was an echo that would mingle with the world's untold stories, changing pace, changing meaning. The price was heavier than ever, but they could no longer pretend the door was closed. This escape was the hinge on which the next story would swing—raw and open, edged with danger but shimmering with the chance to finally discover the whole, cold, fearless truth.

The air around them felt almost tight enough to snap as the two enemies stared each other down in the half-light of the warehouse, the faint rattle of tires on pavement the only other noise in the room. Each of them had been moulded by years of training; their eyes locked, every heartbeat felt like a gunshot. The city's protector stood like a stone wall, and the cloaked shape in front of him gave off a cold, hungry darkness. Everything they each cared about balanced on the next breath, and neither would turn away. The silence buzzed, electric, as they began to circle, each daring the other to take a first, telling step. The clock slowed to a crawl; the warehouse walls felt like they wanted to fold in, trapping them both. A thin line of sweat traced the hero's forehead; the other's breath hissed out in slow, steady gulps. Time had narrowed to this one heartbeat, the single instant that would decide who rose and who vanished. Then, in a flash brighter than a storm, the other exploded forward, and the night shattered into fists and feet. The hero's body remembered every drill; his hands moved faster than thought, blocking each blow with the blade of his forearms and the heel of his boot. They carved a brutal, humming rhythm through the space, every impact like thunder, every dodge a whisper of air that could mean life or death.

They fought with their bodies and their minds. Every punch and every dodge was a test, probing for the chink that would crack the other. Minutes merged into forever. The roar of their blood drowned everything else, turning the cold, rust-echoing warehouse into a spinning blur of fists and fire. Victory was a cliff both of them clung to, clawing with every ounce of muscle and marrow. Each faint, every hammering hit, every well-timed slip was choreographed ruthlessness. The set of their jaws, the steel in their eyes, spoke louder than the bruises. As the fight climbed to its peak, the air crackled like a thunderhead. Blows and shouts collided hard enough to rattle the rafters, and the warehouse itself seemed to pulse. Neither contestant flinched, sheer stubborn fire shoving them past the smoke and the sting. In that one heartbeat, their true colours bared themselves; futures balanced on a razor's edge. Then, in a blink that stretched like a month, the world tipped. One quick, brutal motion shattered the stand-off, sending a shudder that would slam past these four walls and into everyone waiting outside.

The hero saw a gap, a flash of chance, and lunged, flipping the fight around with a move that shocked the shadow he faced. For a long heartbeat, neither of them made a sound; only the rushing of blood and the heavy slaps of their lungs broke the quiet. When the dust finally drifted down, it showed the hero standing tall, courage and a quick brain tipping the fight in his favour. Panting, he looked over the ruined space, knowing he had only bought a moment's cheer. The bigger storm still loomed, so he tightened his grip and pictured the road ahead, the flash of their fierce clash pushing him forward on the endless chase for justice.

Agent Miller and his crew crept closer, nerves knife-sharp, the unknown spot glowing on their screens like a broken thorn. Bit by quiet bit, the map had unfolded, and now every footstep on the cold concrete of the place felt like nudging a sleeping wasp. One slip, one wrong shout, and the world may tip. The price of failure was the colour of flags and borders.

Through the twisting halls, panic pushed them faster with

every step. They arrived in the final chamber, smoke-black and humming with hidden machines. Bright towers of tech cast sharp shadows, and a ring of steely soldiers guarded the prize. Moving like ghosts, the squad slipped nearer, every breath measured. Then, out of the gloom, the enemy stepped into view. The same shadow that had slipped through every trap for a decade. Minutes dragged like sticky clock hands, and the air sharpened with danger. Agent Miller scanned the console arrays, and a fragile sparkle in the panels snagged his stare—one tiny shard of proof that could shatter the whole lie. The sight jolted the squad like fresh coffee, sparking the wildfire of hope they had chased for months.

Following the trail, they uncovered a lattice of hidden cells, dark ships, and masked servers spreading like ink storms over oceans. The web was tighter, wider, and filthier than they had imagined. Once the picture settled in their minds, the magnitude of the fight settled on their shoulders like iron. Agent Miller felt the heavy brand of duty, and he knew every heartbeat of his team now pulsed in the same thunderous measure.

With grit and grit alone, they shoved the pieces of the puzzle together under the flickering lights of the old safe house. One truth after another fell into place, and the cruel engine behind the chaos flickered into view. At the axle of it all, a name whispered only behind sealed lips: a faceless puppeteer whose reach stretched into shadows where most dared not look. Yet, every answered question came strapped with its own knife; the closer they crept to the truth, the darker the road became. Within the storm, friend became foe and foe became friend; promises were branded on the heart, and a new price was placed on every life. Still, the night dragged on, dragging roots into the earth, pushing them toward a storm that none would tame. That final snap of insight sent currents of chaos that would uproot every tower of stone and steel, tip the scales between the meek and the mighty, and summon a day when the whole earth would catch its breath.

As they pressed further through the underworld of shadows, a silent lane of lights began to glow, and it wound straight toward the restless belly of Lagos.

The team recoiled when they learned a top-level inside operative had slipped past security inside one of Nigeria's most guarded agencies. Shock morphed into racing adrenaline when their deadlines collapsed; fresh evidence testified that this rot spread well beyond Nigeria's borders. Now everyone's breath smelled of gunpowder. Trust shrank like ice under a midday sun. Once-bright allies became shadows; every smile was a trap, every loud thud of a door a possible red line. Reports that had once felt like checkmate opened new trap doors, rerouting the investigation into darker lanes. Safeguards, safe houses, friends—each faded into question marks. Just when the light almost winked out, an unsigned message pulse-buzzed into one eager hand. The signature cypher—shredded into rings of the same punishing math—stale, and centuries old. Follow the bread crumbs, the paper dared, and a ghost known only as the Melkite Avenger would turn the lock. The clock, a merciless metronome, guzzled seconds while the lights flickered. Racing through alleyways and forgotten mainframes, they chased a growing fire that crowded inside their chests. One wrong turn and empires might smoulder. Ethical map-points shifted under the boot of necessity; every sacrifice felt like carving anew into their own skins. But surrender, they knew, meant watching the world fracture.

The terrifying truth they stumbled upon changed everything, dragging them into a twisted web of lies and hidden power where every face wore a mask. With each thread they tugged, danger coiled tighter, and betrayal loomed like a thundercloud. Still, they refused to turn back. They steeled themselves for the decisive blow, fully aware that the only path to victory was riddled with traps. This discovery would redraw the map of global espionage and rewrite their deepest beliefs, creating a legend that would be told for generations to come.

A thick silence wrapped around the team as they readied themselves for the last, decisive fight. They had faced every imaginable setback, but this—the end of the line—was the moment they had trained for. Each obstacle had sharpened their focus and convinced them that quitting was never an option. Stepping through the shattered gates of the lonely compound, every nerve felt ignited. Faint footfalls bounced off the concrete halls, reminding them what was at stake. The leader, jaw set and eyes glinting like flint, raised the signal for caution. With guarded steps, they advanced, heartbeats in octave, breath as quiet as the dark.

Out of the shadows, a figure stepped forward. Dark armour gleamed, and every inch of the silhouette crackled with authority and danger. This was the puppet master of every hardship they'd endured, the spectre they'd chased from one continent to the next. Words snapped between them, terse and charged, the echoes of old collisions still ringing in every syllable. Tension rippled through the room, growing hotter with every breath, the stakes climbing higher until victory and defeat felt like a single heartbeat away. Two forces squared off, and in that heartbeat, the world levelled itself. Adrenaline ripened into fire, and the conflict moved like a tightly wound spring, every strike choreographed, every dodge a heartbeat of maths. It was a test of iron wills and sharper minds; one fraction of a second out of place, and everything would shatter. Through the pressure, their bond glittered like a sharpened blade. Each teammate played their role to perfection, bodies and tactics weaving a single, fluid counterstrike against the enemy's cold brilliance. A thousand odds stacked like storm clouds over them, but resolve flared, a candle against the gale, forging their steadiness. Silence thickened until it hurt, split only by the sound of laboured breaths and the distant whisper of steel against steel.

Time hung like a held breath as they strained against each other, the end balanced on a razor edge. In a heartbeat, the hero lunged for the single gap of weakness, a gamble that rippled the tide of the fight. A wild tide of motion spilt out, the long-promised finish flaring to life like a struck fuse, their pulses drumming like war drums beside the plains of dirt. When the final act stepped forward, every fight, every scar, every whispered fear spun into one singular, blinding light. Thunder of the clash rolled away across the hollow reaches, closing a long road and opening a wild, fresh dawn.

The room was a sealed vault, quiet enough to hear a dying breath, while the two stood like storm clouds waiting to break. Inside, every locked vault of feeling twisted and twisted. They had climbed to this razor lip of decision, and the ripple of their move would outlive them both. One man wore his courage like armour, gaze fixed and hard; the other, a still flame of inward strength. Nations balanced on the thin edge of their hands, and the weight of that truth sank like a stone into their chests.

Still, under every glare and every sour word, a thin line of respect refused to snap. They had both walked the same aching road to this hour; the fights, the flags, the burning cities had bled into one long final scar, and whatever was decided in the next heartbeat would steer a million lives. A stillness so tight it hurt was split by one short, terrible line of speech. Its answer, hush now, could mean returning to gardens or turning the world to ash. They felt the weight of it in the marrow of their bones. When they answered, the echoes would drown the stone and steel of the war room. While they weighed the moment, flashes of old battles replayed—blooded victories, whispered betrayals, the cold bite of loss, the slip of forgiveness. Every chapter of their years had twisted into the other, a tangled braid they could never cut free of. Now, at the gunpoint of fate, they faced the same dark, wide enemy. In the gloom of every doubt, a thin spark of light still trembled, offering smiles of tomorrows they had never planned. Inside, the war never left. Duty wrestled with conscience, both snarling and bruised. The room throbbed with unspoken terrors and quiet dreams. Beneath gold braid and scarred skin, they all carried the same shame and the same hunger, scared the leash might snap, and their souls might tumble into the abyss past for-giveness.

Their fates were bound to cross, and where they did, the moment born of a hundred crossroad moments took real, fateful shape. Seconds added themselves to the room, indif-ferent to the heavy, weighing silence that begged for pause. Each tick contradicted the hopes and fears that had stormed the hearts of those present. The world beyond the door went on, unaware of the hurricane building there, yet the world already bore the faintest tremors of the choice still unsung. At last, a steady breath and steady voice pushed one word across the table, dissolving the gridlock and remaking the hour. The word lingered, and across the table a quiet bow of the head passed between sworn rivals—both knowing, in the marrow of the moment, that the coming days would carry the same weight for either side. The coin had rolled, the coin had rolled, the coin had rolled, and in the pure finality of that single breath, the map of what was yet to come was forever, painfully rewritten.

Part Three

The Global Kill Switch

Chapter One

The Choice

Nova and Kofi sat in the grey hush of the small room, the air thick with unspoken dread. They had built their lives on firm principles, but those principles now collided with the fragile order of the entire globe. They were at a moral crossroads, a decision looming that could alter the course of history. Every second felt like an hour, every breath a step deeper into the dark, as they wrestled with a decision that dwarfed all they had ever known. Kofi stared at the table, the skin between his brows pulled tight, the flicker of his gaze revealing a storm of questions. Years of negotiating had sharpened his mind, but tonight the sharpest knife was his own conscience. If they held the line they had always held, would the future burn too brightly for any flag of those beliefs to fly? Or was the wiser cruelty the crueller mercy, a snuffing out of small ideals for the broad flame of collective safety?

Across the table, Nova's restlessness was small but telling. The flat of her palm pressed into the table to steady the slight shake, as if her body could anchor her spirit. Justice had been her North Star, a guiding light seen at every post and every dark hour, yet that same light now refracted into vague colours that did not add to white. She could picture the decision spreading out like ripples on a river, touching borders yet unguarded, lives yet unbroken. The tension hung between them, a stretched thread that would, at last, be pulled. Whatever the answer, they would weave it into the loom of history, and the loom would never forget.

The steady buzz of the air conditioner throbbed against the hush that wrapped them like an old blanket. Outside, the sun kept its schedule, shining on the streets and the people who never knew how close the river of history had come to changing course within these four blank walls. The moment tugged, unintended, into long still minutes, and Nova and Kofi exchanged the only language they had left: quiet, true and terrible. The miles they had marched for separate flags had never seemed separate until now. Each of them had sworn to keep the world's delicate gear turning, yet tonight that same gear waited for a turn only they could give. What they fought for had become the very thing they now hesitated to serve. Breach it, and the whole wide future could tilt. Kofi's shoulders fell at last, and his breath broke the stillness like the first crack of thunder.

"This cannot be a fight for names on lists," he said, and the calm in his voice felt like a distant echo. "It is the very frame we have promised to hold."

Nova followed his gaze, her own steady yet submerged.

"And the price for that frame?" she answered, so quiet that the walls almost swallowed the question.

The answer to both hearts lingered, a dark shape crowding the things they had vowed never to forsake.

The path ahead asked more than they'd ever had to give—more than sacrifice. It asked the hope of generations, the name by which the future would remember them.

In the shadow of her cluttered room, Elena's breath felt thin. The note from New York had dropped like a stone, sending the whole plan spinning. Once, sacrifice had felt like a choice; now it felt like a currency. The hour of twilight held her gaze, and the skyline looked like a trembling heartbeat. She knew the hourglass was almost empty and the grains had names—names she'd carried like charms. Her breath hitched, and she picked up the phone, palm wet against the cool plastic. Memories of the red-led offices, of floors buzzing between fact and rumour, chased each other in circles. With each tone that sounded, she counted the seconds she would never get back. When the final ring became a hush, she asked for him—an echo from the tunnels, the name of a man who wore loyalty like a disguise.

The voice was static and smoke; she spoke faster than she

thought, and colour fled her cheeks. She crafted a bargain, a price that ground her heart to powder, yet in the same twist of breath she felt it could be a bridge—fragile, trembling, yet wide enough to carry a future.

When she pressed the phone's button, and it went quiet, a cold wave rippled along her spine. The conversation had invited her into the silent layer of espionage, a place where every whispered promise shackled her future. The line she'd crossed was one of the most careful negotiators would ignore. Her heart raced as she replayed the secret that now lived inside her, a secret that could potentially betray her colleagues and her cause. Yet somewhere behind her ribs, a small flame whispered that maybe peace needed this small betrayal.

The hands of the clock crawled while she wore the floor to shards beneath her feet. Guilt and iron purpose wrestled inside her, each kneeing the other harder. She replayed the risks until they felt like shards stuck in her throat. But with every heavy breath, her spine went straighter. She would finish what she had begun, no matter what price the finish would ask. The moment the candle guttered, she drew her notes and charts, breath held like a bird, ready to unfold the tomorrow she had now designed.

Because she understood the soft truth of the dark: inside the murky corridors of nations, decisions wore no clear colours and hope often whispered in the same voice as betrayal.

With each breath she took, she readied herself for the next bold move, her heart locked against the rough tide she must cross, a tide filled with the shadows and lies of espionage, sharper than blades. She was aware that the path she had picked carried these dangers, but she was determined to see it through.

In a shadowed office, the flickering light of the screens

painted his face with a cold, blue glow that matched the cold edge in his gaze. Data coiled around him like a silken net—trade flows, diplomatic pings, and the silent drift of the men and women whose choices shaped the world's edge. Leader of a watches-with-silence arm, Omar lived inside the storm of numbers. His brain hummed with the sting of every threat and the cold whip of every warning. For him, a balance sheet was not a sheet but an atlas of souls, a map of secrets, a ledger of the flicker that divides friend from shadow. He replayed the voices from the field, spinning their bleached, re-ordered syllables until the truth surfaced, impossibly pale yet clear. Each fragment, every glint of light caught in the night air, risked tipping the world from brittle peace to a roar of flames. Omar understood that the rooms where decisions dressed in silk could wound oceans and uncoil histories. His diagrams married sine waves and probabilities to the pulse of kissing trust, the sharp crack of betrayal, the brittle laughter of a fragile pact.

With every tap on the keyboard, he plunged deeper into the shadows, mapping the hidden dreams and darker wishes of the players who walked the fragile wire of world power. Then, inside the whirl of locked messages and muffled exchanges, Omar felt a tremor—a faint crack in the surface that whispered of a distant, gathering tempest. His gut, sharpened by a decade of following whispered clues through tangled nightmares, warned him that the moment for a bold move was slipping into view. The risks were towering, and the result would carve the future of entire peoples. He poured over the columns of data, untangling the riddle of colliding designs, and the weight of what he might soon unleash settled like molten metal in his chest. His reading would slide through the pipes of capitals and land in the hands of kings, of shopkeepers, of mothers tucking in their kids. The cold truth that so much was balanced on his verdict daunted a fierce promise: nothing would be missed, no faint flicker ignored. Hours blurred into the dark, and the coffee cooled into silence. At last, Omar pushed away from the desk, the chill of the metal still a nerve twitch. He looked up with eyes of sharpened iron. He had pulled on a strand that knotted what had seemed to be stray threads into a single rope leading to one terrible, crucial insight.

This discovery would peel away the layers of falsehood and expose the real actors hiding in the shadows. As Omar finalised his report for the secret council charged with guiding his unit, he felt the air grow heavy with the coming storm. The decisions he would soon deliver could rewrite the rules of the game, and he alone had the evidence to nudge the balance either toward small order or screaming anarchy.

The air inside the marble corridors of the United Nations felt electric with dread the day the Final Demand was announced. Diplomats and ministers, pale and restless, recognised the truth etched in their calendars: whichever way the next few days unfolded, the world would bend a different way inside the vast, echoing assembly chamber, flags from distant capitals arrayed like nervous sentinels, while the tense conversations of a hundred tongues seemed to vibrate with the same silent prayer. Beyond closed doors, the negotiations blazed hotter than hopeful law. Hands pointed to the unreadable clock, its harsh ticks marking a countdown to choices that would not forgive. The Secretariat's position was sharp as shrapnel: the terms admitted no equivocation, and the response expected no delay.

Global leaders now stood on a fragile line, every choice they made rippling into a future they could not see. To Kofi, the deadline was more than a demand; it was a test of his moral core. A man who had always walked the tightrope of honesty, he now felt the razor edge between the orders he must follow and the justice he could not betray. Heavy clouds of doubt thickened in his mind—was acquiescence weakness, was resistance rebellion? The answer determined more than policy; it could determine millions of lives. The weight of every last one pressed hard and bitterly on his back.

Around him, the quiet hum of quiet disloyalty spread like wildfire at night. Reading rooms and corridors had become spider webs of hidden treaties and half-muttered threats, each strand tightening just enough to make the whole fragile structure shudder. Beneath the polite smiles and clipped signatures, true motives slipped like knives; fragile balances no longer felt stable, and every shift of a seat felt like a till on a scale.

As the clock approached the final chime, the silhouette of war stood uppermost on the skyline—dark, silent, and full of hunger. The marred past of treaties broken and families shattered now pooled in one last powder keg, and the spark hovered just within reach. The planet held its breath—one word, one move away from a blaze that could consume everything it had spent centuries trying to rebuild.

Veiled threats brushed against quiet promises in a dangerous waltz, every slip a warning that rippled through the polished chambers of diplomacy. Here, in the charged air, the futures of entire nations dangled from a thread so thin it might snap at any heartbeat. Whatever decisions the diplomats crafted beneath the blue dome would carve an irreversible path for the species, leading either to lasting light or final darkness. The moment was the crucible itself, the forge that would test the world's weary spirit, placing the weight of tomorrow on the straight backs of a few.

Beneath the thrum of New York traffic, farther down than most lifts dare descend, a matchup of minds was unfolding in the charcoal underbelly of the United Nations. The board was every continent, and the pawns were soldiers, oil, and quiet votes from places so small you couldn't find them on a tourist map. Rumours of a phantom, a double agent wearing the organisation's blue press card, slipped from office to office like a chill wind, turning open handshakes into tight fists. Clocks ticked louder than speakers in the chapel, and at every summit, the glow of a red button hovered above the delegates, warning that miscalibrated diplomacy might soon become irretrievable death. Ever since the founding charter was inked, loyalty within the UN had flickered like the amber of an old bulb, illuminating faces, then gutters, then faces again.

The shocking news of a traitor inside the United Nations blasted apart the fragile trust that had once held the world together. Who the double agent was, nobody could say. Moving among diplomats with ease, the shape-shifting spy tugged invisible strings, steering decisions from the shadows. Scuttlebutt in the dim hallways spoke of buried scandals and secret pacts born amid guns and smoke. Suddenly, the fate of nations swung like a tightrope, and every person under the UN roof became a suspect under a cold, bright spotlight. Friends were now ranked as possible turncoats, and even the smallest comment felt as heavy as a loaded gun. Away from the cameras, quiet nets of investigators were cast, slowly snagging lies that had drifted together like drifting smoke. Each fresh catch jolted every file and every handshake with new voltage. While the crisis tightened its noose, the double agent drifted like a rumour, stitching a grim quilt of half-truths and false alarms. The talk in the grand hall rose to a fever, curling the air with anxiety. Hunt teams raced deeper every hour, chasing an escalating story of secret tunnels, bitter betrayals, and cold-eyed ambition that would stop at nothing.

Right now, peace hangs by a thread, and you can't tell a friend from a hidden enemy. Every tiny action now feels like it could tip history over the edge, because a double-cross in the United Nations would unlock nightmares no one can picture. One hidden saboteur moves from hallway to hallway, a ghost that chills the last truce. The seconds keep ticking toward midnight, and everyone keeps still, hearts pounding on the fragile edge of what tomorrow might still break.

Inside the dim safe house, a lone lamp flickers over Nova, casting long, trembling shadows across the small wooden table. Her eyes, dark like an unfurling storm, stare at the surface as if it might hold the answers she craves. After a long silence, she finally breaks it, her voice like moth wings brushing against the house's quiet.

"Didn't think it would end like this, with every bond turned to wire and every truth to smoke. Duty at my back, justice whispering in my ear, and the road ahead soaked in the dark. Every stride peels another sliver from the shield of who I was, until all that's left feels like the echo of a name I barely own."

The weariness in her tone answers the small space like an old wound. Nova unfolds the memory of the months that led her here, and the picture turns kaleidoscopic: every face a mask, every promise a thread wound tighter. She describes the long, bruising hours spent weaving the lie that keeps her alive, all while the mirror asks the same question: what line is left to cross before the girl in it is no longer her?

Her voice peels back the layers she usually keeps locked up like folded paper inside her chest. Each confession drops like a stone, sinking into the hush, the syllables heavy with nights she never named. Still, underneath the ache, there's a fierce spark, a refusal to let the darkness swallow her whole. Every syllable is folded with the same steel she carries into the fire. She is hunting the truth, and the quiet room keeps step with her search, crafting the shape of a woman who will not let circumstance define her. Minute by minute, her words blur the bright lines between what the law calls right and what the heart knows is safe. She pleads for a second chance, and the sound ripples beyond the barred windows, past the walls that usually swallow secrets. In her voice, you can still hear the human will that keeps stitching itself together, even when the stitches are on fire. When her final sentence hushes, the night itself feels thinner. Nova pushes back her chair and stands, straight-backed, her eyes like twin lanterns on a fresh trail. In that held-breath pause, a fresh, clear design heats the map of her face, revealing the next corner in the impossible road she keeps walking.

Kofi watched the holographic chart swirl over his desk, bright lines of data like tangling wires, and felt the room close in. A single choice, his choice, could redraw the map of nations, and the pressure clawed the back of his throat. He had worn his loyalty to the UN like a second skin, proud and unyielding, yet now, the sentry of secrets, he stood at the cliff's edge of conscience. As Director of Strategic Operations, he carried files sealed with the weight of silence; the words inside could nudge the quiet throats of missiles and set the world ever so slightly off its axis. Duty sang in his ear, yet the price of that obedience slipped like smoke through his fingers. He paused, forcing himself to remember why he had walked through the UN's wide glass doors years ago: a dream of one shared peace, a dream bright enough to blind. Now, inside the shaded corridors of power, the dream felt thinner; behind the polished marble, he saw the gears that turned behind layers of deception, and he wondered if the light had ever been more than a mask.

In the hushed corners of his office, Kofi fought an uneasy silence. Dim screens pulsed pale blue, tracing anxious portraits across his own face as he weighed the fallout of what he might choose next. In the half-light of espionage, the lines between duty and conscience dissolved, loyalty and justice, once clear, slipped beneath doubt's rising tide. The weight of that evening's verdict pressed his convictions like fragile glass. His stare fell on the still photo of Elena, the agent whose heart seemed hidden beneath her code name. Every move she made sent tremors through capitals and corridors, and Kofi felt her next decision would tip the scales. The longer he studied her, the stronger the prickle of intuition: she was playing a longer game, one he could not yet read. Outside, shadows swirled across the walls, the office clock ticking like a heartbeat counting down. Kofi felt the seconds pull at him. Silence held him tightly, and finally, with one slow, steady breath, he released the tension into a choice that would change everything.

He would blaze a trail that mocked tradition, a trail that moved beyond duty and straight into audacious will. The choices were made, and Kofi readied himself for the storm that would follow his daring leap. In the secret world where power and shadows mingle, loyalties would bend, crack, and shatter. With one purposeful step into the void, he braced for the rough road ahead, already hearing the thunder of his choice roll through the ages.

Kofi's choice echoed through the cramped, half-lit safe space where the weight of empires rested on worn shoulders. The furious clatter of keyboards surged as the crew surged into high gear, rushing to stitch together scraps of truth gathered through long months of sleepless nights. Every click pulled them a little nearer to the brink, yet doubt hovered like cold breath on skin. Stilling the swirl of nerves, Nova anchored herself, face set like iron. Her eyes darted across the shifting screens that traced the world's veins, and her brain hunted for the one missing piece that could shift the game.

The moment hung over them like a thunderstorm: lose now, and everything crumbles. Hours folded into each other, and the complicated plan started to settle like a net cast over a churning sea. If all went well, it would snag the sharks of power now circling the globe and pull them underwater. Success. Every silent heart in the room kept counting down the seconds. Omar, the ghost dressed in grey whose voice was rarely heard, was the mind behind the wave. Colleagues already called him 'The Architect' for stitching victories where others saw ashes. He walked a narrow strip of the floor, sorry boards creaking beneath him, while his thoughts ricocheted like lasers, bouncing through systems and contradictions. Each new path of fate was already folded and pocketed. He could almost taste the paradox of pressure and calm. Somewhere in the dark, Elena already ghosted through the first sealed door, her silhouette a promise inside a promise. Danger hung in rings around her, yet her pulse kept a metronome faster than fear. She was the only lock that could crack this vault.

As they waited for her life-saving signal, the still air in the command room felt charged, and every heartbeat whispered, "come home." Somewhere far above, corridors of power whispered treachery and shifting loyalties, the map of options twisting into a gauntlet that could crack the world open. The UN's clock ticked above every conversation, a burning fuse over fragile lines of conversation. To ignore it flirted with fire; to bow was to cut the thread of everything they had called justice. Principle or survival—one choice, a single line in the record of centuries. So the last night ordered itself into dawn, a hush before the next storm. The new mission, forged in smoke and regret, cooled by iron purpose, carried the weight of every fragile hope. The hour of decisions had come, and among the whirlpools of nations, a calculated storm was about to sing.

Under the pale watch of the moon, the old warehouse waited like a grave. In its bones, the team moved, faces wrapped in darkness.

Nova made sure everyone had gear that melted into the night. The air hummed with the kind of silence only great danger invites. Tonight, they were finally going after the fortress the whole world dreaded. Every foot of ground had been sized and measured. The crossing point, the corridors inside, the storage wings—Omar had peeled the walls apart with drones and satellites, stitching back the images into maps that pulsed like hearts. Elena ran her fingers along her comm gear, the signals slicing the still air with beeps that only she could hear. Her eyes were hard and bright, the same eyes that had never flinched when she slid under fences to lift weapons away. Kofi hovered over the blueprints, the glow of the pad casting ghostly shapes across his face as he erased a guard route here and printed a new sensor blind spot there. The UN's ultimatum still raced through the news, a countdown tattooed across the planet, and their harder answer now lived inside them: this night, or never. When they reached the fortress, every footfall whispered like a breath slowing into still water. They moved as one, every tilt of shoulders and shift of weight a note in the same song, the song of people who had rehearsed their act until it ceased to be practice and became promise.

The tower rose like a fate-worn watchman, its dark walls harbouring a promise of hell. Still, they walked forward, resolve burning hotter than fear. The journey's opening stride doubled as its deadliest, yet retreat had already drowned in their own noise. The task required grit that would not bend and minds that already danced with risk. When they crossed the outer ring, the hush of the night tore open under the thunder of their entry. Slipping through the heart of the enemy's stronghold, they had trained a lifetime for the order. All the signals, the soft crackle of speech in throat mikes and the shy pulse of gadgets, voiced how heavy the night really was. Each step whispered louder than the last, lifting the fate of the whole world on the arch of their boots. Passing the threshold was not sweat-strained inches of flesh; it was the mark of devotion bottled and blown back again—faith in one another, spirit that laughed at ruin.

Woven into midnight's dark cloak, they glided toward the outer wall, every heartbeat a secret of its own.

Nova's crew had schemed every turn and every switch, flipping every crack in the enemies' defences into a doorway for themselves. Greased with nerves, they slid through ring after ring of alarms and guards, the smell of burnt nerves in the air. If they slipped, the world would shatter. They slipped through the first blue light, snuffing cameras like birthday candles and ghosting motion strips as easily as the wind. The enemy's husk loomed like a marbled rock cliff, but Nova's keep-eating-glass resolve pushed them step by step into the black. Feet marked charts in the air; every heartbeat, every gamble, landed like a loaded die. The centre of the ghost thumped ahead, a place where shadow kissed both dagger and diamond. Beyond the guards, Elena slipped into the backbone of the place, the classified hive. Her fingers streaked over ghosted keys, the light singing like trapped rain. Firewalls melted under the warm hush of her will. While she drew blueprints of the enemies' intestines, Omar and his shadow section fired the missiles: flickering drones and sound shells that screamed in the wrong hangars. The false Odysseys drifted, glittering like poisoned chocolate, buying them the precious heartbeat they needed.

They spiralled down through the underbelly of the complex, a chill in the air that smelled like hidden schemers at work. Nova sharpened every nerve, sensing danger before it arrived. Just as the watchful spotlights were about to catch them, a quick dodge passed the guards from one door to the next like a tossed coin. Margins of luck had narrowed to the blade of a knife, and the only way to win was to move as one under the eyes of a dozen foes. At last, they stood before the last door, the pulse that held the whole web together. When Kofi stepped forward, the team held its breath. He pressed the charge, and the wall blew inward with a hiss and a breath of darkness. They slipped through the hush into the very throat of the lion, where secrets were born and swallowed. Every breath said the same thing: nothing would ever be the same again. Time turned rubbery, stretching and snapping, until the glow of the hard drives cut the hush. They leaned close, and the screens spilt the blueprints of disaster—every jagged line a threat to the world above. They downloaded the files into waiting drives, a flood of data now safely in their hands, and for a heartbeat, the glow of the success drowned the risk that had chased them from the first breath of the night.

Yet, their victory didn't last long; the hard clatter of boots against the stone floor rang out, shattering the stillness and warning they had run out of time.

Chapter Two

The Trojan Horse

The crew slips through the shadowy aisles, moving like whispers, knowing that one misplaced footfall might set off sirens loud enough to summon every guard in the building. Each footfall lands in the same quiet, every inhale feels like a held secret. They are burning the seconds behind them, because every lost second tightens the crisis. The thrum of stacked servers cradles them in cold air, guiding them to the centre of the data vault. What began as a hush-hush op has exploded into a sprint against a hidden enemy who seems to breathe in every dark doorway. Tension stretches between them like a wire as they flash quick looks, sharing whole plans in the space between blinks. They have run drills for this, polished every lock-pick and sprint, armoured their minds against doubt. Yet, drills do not sharpen a heart for the moment when everything tips. The moment they clear the last aisle, the weight of the room presses like a stone. This is far beyond a stolen blueprint or hidden camera; it is a clash for the pulse of a planet's worth of data. With entire futures riding on their wires, they have to move needle-precise, aware that one wrong flick could drown the whole world in chaos.

Every careful stride they take whispers a mixture of caution and iron will, their eyes gleaming with a promise they mean to keep no matter what. Under the thin, flickering lights of the server aisles, the quiet throb of machines and the heat of their determination fuse into a single, charged heartbeat. Outside their narrow bubble, shadowless predators are already closing in, their unseen plans already drawing a map of conflict that will shatter the net and echo into the future. Beneath the polished quiet of the data centre, a storm of hidden motives spins faster with each heartbeat, waiting to explode in a measured storm of noise and truth.

Tension shimmered in the chill air as they steeled themselves for the last fight. Before them, a shimmering maze of steel and wires pulsed with the secrets they needed. Every footfall bounced dully off distant walls, a drumbeat of the size of what they had to finish. Descending deeper into the frozen stronghold, their parted breaths braided with the steady thrum of the racks, weaving a strange, cold music that neither encouraged nor cared whether they danced to its tune.

Finally, they stood in the digital heart, the pulse of the whole system. Data shot through this space like bright streams of mercury, carrying the enemy's secrets. Without a single word wasted, they unpacked their precision gear, ready to unleash their rehearsed assault. Screen lights pulsed like strobe flares as they wrestled past firewalls and mazes, every keystroke tightening the noose around the truth they craved. But the shadow across the wire taught caution. They bored deeper, only to find barrier after barrier, each growing stronger, each coded in fresh dread. Wits crashed against code in a cruel test of brains, a chase where every byte trembled like glass over the edge. Heartbeats synced with the ticking clock, a blade of chance dangling by a single vector. Then, the quiet exploded. An alarm screamed, bright and furious, warning that they were no longer ghosts. Instant retribution rammed down the wire, an avalanche of scripts and failsafes, each meant to crush, to break, to bury the daring.

But the squad had foreseen this moment and rallied with iron wills, driving themselves past limits the body should never breach, reclaiming the cyber sky bit by blazing bit. Seconds lengthened into minutes, minutes swirled into hours—an unbroken cyclone of strike and shield. Each tap of the key carried trembling risk, every choice poised between the gold of triumph and the ashes of ruin. Pressure hummed between them, hot and living, as if the air itself whispered that fate was watching.

Then, when despair hugged them like ink, a single spark

flared. Block by block, shield by shield, the opponent's wall gave way beneath the tide of the squad's sharper minds and steadier hearts. The current shifted, and the edge of triumph glowed ahead, a roaring blaze that scorched the frost of doubt and fear.

At last, the victory was more than circuitry won; it was proof that the human spirit—when forged by fire—can defy anything once thought unbreakable.

When they finally pushed the heavy doors of the data centre open and stepped into the humid outside night, bone-deep fatigue pressed on their shoulders. Still, the spark of victory was a steady fire in their chests. They had rewritten every unspoken rule of cyber warfare, and the echoes of their gamble would outlive clouds of obsolete code drifting into nothing.

The Data Centre towered over the city, a sparkling wedge of glass hiding its pulsing, humming heart. Inside, the cool thrum of fans and the slow dance of red and green lights held the city's secrets, and inside the heartbeat of the city, a quiet storm was found. The six figures glided along rubber-black floors, shadows inside shadows, and every muted footfall tightened the air like a drawstring. One hallway, another corner, and they would reach the core, the place where their enemy's dark, glittering dream was about to wake. Trapped in the amber glow of conduits, the lead agent held up a hand. One by one, they sank behind a waist-high white rack and pressed to the glass.

Across the chamber, the glass walls burned blue, and one shape stood alone, backlit by the skyline of circuits and stars. The person they'd chased, the fate-written ghost, was half outline and half cobra, facing a constellation of humming screens that flared brighter with every beat of the city.

The moment had come to act. Every second of practice paid off as the team moved like a synchronised clock. Security gates gave way, walls of fire crumbled, and tangled codes folded like paper. Yet, when the prize glittered ahead, the awful truth shot through the air: they were walking into a trap. A silhouette stepped forward, the glow of the screens sharpening its grin. A calm voice began to spin a story that peeled back layers they had never known, revealing a blueprint invisible yet everywhere, a scheme buried deep inside every network, every server, every cable. This was the final card, a move so grand its ripples could realign borders and balance sheets with a single stroke. Shock gave way to fury. The team dove into the code as if its lines were the very heartbeat of the planet. Data clashed like swords in a storm. A single character typed, a single signal blocked, could tip futures like pennies off a table. The monitors throbbed, shadowing faces tense with courage and fire. They were no longer fighters; they were architects of tomorrow, carving space for choice in a code-written fate.

Like clockwork, the seconds fell away, each tap of the key pushing the truth nearer to the surface. From his little glass bubble, Roger fought the same private war as every sleepless soul in the sector. It was a stream of code and steel nerves, a collision of wits flaring across the wires. For a moment, the balance wavered like spun glass, shuddering between wins and losses, and the current began to bend his way.

He poured everything into the stroke, and with that one unholy blast, the enemy's glittering walls cracked. Their vaunted vault—cold, black, and boastfully sleek—bowed outward, and the sacrifice of every midnight prayer was repaid in sparks. One last hammering wave and the heart of their hoax lay naked, thrumming for the whole globe to scan. The balance of shadows and fire tipped hard, the leader's overconfidence lay bare, and the last trap collapsed into legend. Roger and his team straightened, badges smeared with burnt caffeine and triumph, eyes already scanning for the next horizon, already hungry for the next horizon, already hungry for the next horizon.

Roger eased back, chair creaking under the tired weight of ten years. His eyes stayed locked on the big black screen, the glow washing his face in ghostfire, tracing the grooves of a face that had never learned to bend.

He inhaled, every nerve buzzing with the tight snap of the moment he'd worked his whole life to reach. The glowing code spread out in front of him was more than light; it was the final stretch of the race. Slashing through his mind came memories of late nights chasing numbers and pixels, every line of script a thread in the same dark cloak. Truth was his fuel, a fire he never let die. The steady thrum of the servers thrummed under his ribcage, a heartbeat of silicon and promise. He felt the weight of what lay inside each spinning fan—the same force that made cities tremble and empires crack. The same force that, until now, had slipped through the fingers of men he respected. But Roger had never confused might with choice. Power was a voice that could roar or whisper, and he planned to sing the right song. Alone in the chill of the data shack, his thoughts settled into an iron line. He had peeled back the curtain on a shadow that had crept across every border, a poison steady and dark enough to drown a whole world. Finger raised above the keys, he let the next command slice into the lie, one sturdy rip after another, until the bright truth was the only thing left standing.

The truth pressed heavily on him, lighting a fire inside that would not die. Yet when the weight of what he knew sank in, a cold, creeping dread wrapped around his heart. He possessed the truth, yet he stood alone against a ruthless enemy. The size of what he had to do towered before him, darkening the edge of his courage. He sifted through images of loss, trading his comfort in exchange for safety. Inside the buzz of the routers and the hum of power supplies, Roger made his vow in silence. He would be the watchman who refused to bend, the defiant light when shadows stretched long. Every scrap of skill, every ounce of strength, he would put forth to drag the monsters in the dark into the burning light. The burden of truth had rifled through his life and stripped him of small dreams, replacing them with a stark and heavy calling to guard the fragile tomorrow. He locked his eyes on the endless black of the network and tightened his grip for the fight yet to begin. The chatter of doubt in his mind fell quiet, replaced by the quiet click of a door behind him—the door that led into the oncoming storm.

For the first time in a career shaped by storm after storm, he accepted the burden of real change, ready to reveal secrets designed to rattle the very towers of power. At that instant, the weight of nations balanced in eight frozen seconds, and Roger, alone and unwavering, stood one letter from the fulcrum of the next history.

When the ghost of the speech faded in the remote vault, a chill of warning raced through the operators. They fought back the rising chill, and the lead agent shouted a single command that broke the air like a glass pane. Fingertips hammered the keys, sending the sum of their days racing back at the enemy in disciplined waves of precision. Cool fluorescent bars coloured their faces a ghostly blue inside the black, and every sound of the stroke felt like a footfall in a cathedral. Mutual gaze held, the keystrokes rang with drive against the rising fire. Somewhere miles of racked circuits away, the enemy's own citadel ignited, and scripts met and shattered in grim, beautiful arcs. The quiet room now pulsed, the sole witness the cool hum of turbines and blades straining at the storm.

In the frenzied surge of ones and zeroes, one brilliant crack in the defences sent a jolt of fire through the operatives—ground gained at last, the glimmer of a win in sight. But the brighter the beacon, the darker the shadow; the enemy countered with fresh tricks, jeering as each hard-won inch threatened to vanish. Minute by minute, the climb grew steeper, each pulse of the clock tightening the vice. Then, in the twisting maze of code, new hidden snares sprang to life, and the team hit a storm. Yet in the heart of the storm, the squad's commander spoke, her voice a steel thread pulling every coder back from the brink of doubt and forward to one last, all-or-nothing strike. Fixed on the humming screens, they slipped deeper into the data chasms, seeking cracks wide enough to shim the whole structure while holding back the enemy tide. Waves of adrenaline charged every keystroke; fingers flew in time, the room humming as if one body. Every specialist, helmet-to-helmet, melted doubt into raw volts of will. Pressure pressed like iron, yet they advanced, one laser-lit step at a time. Then they hit the seat of the fortress: a flaw that shimmered like sky through a torn sky. They poured the whole arsenal into that crack. Shock-waves of algorithms tore outward, a ripple that yanked the enemy from its perch, if only for a heartbeat—the heartbeat the team breather muttered into the still air, the heartbeat just enough to turn the tide.

Just when victory felt like it was in their hands, the enemy threw a surprise punch, shattering the operatives' careful plans and planting seeds of doubt over the win they had fought so hard to earn. But they didn't waver. They circled the wagons, read the new enemy play, and charged back into the fight with extra fire and clear purpose. The cramped command centre, already faded by long nights, flickered with new life, its air thick with the grit of people refusing to give in. Intellect met iron will in a struggle that held empires in the balance, driving every member of the team to dig deeper than they knew they could. The minutes slid away, but the steady, rapid tapping of keys kept the world ticking away from darkness.

The clock was running out, and the price of failure was deadly. The team pounded through the tight streets, gunfire cracking like lightning overhead, warning them that death was just one heartbeat away. With every stride, they pressed into the city's dark heart, feeling the heat of the chase pound in their ears. Adrenaline flooded their blood, sharper than the night air, and they inundated through alley after alley, refusing the siren call of fear. Fresh hurdles sprang up with every bend—barriers, agents, traps—but their hearts stayed locked on the one prize that mattered: a crucial piece of evidence that could prevent a catastrophic event. Past cluttered bazaars and lonely wide plazas, the game flew on, and every flash of their target danced just out of capture. The city clenched tighter, every shadow and whisper of wind daring them to quit.

The sun was almost gone, bleeding red across the worn stones, when the chase boiled into its hottest beat. The space between them and their prey shrank like a noose, the wind howled with the promise of victory, and they could almost taste the metal of handcuffs. And then—without warning—a new danger crashed into the game. A web of hidden helpers sprang from the cracks in the city, blocking alleys and corners, their faces familiar and sinister, and the team felt the mission sway like a burning tightrope.

What had started as a simple race against the clock had twisted into a fierce duel of nerves and will. The team shot past tight alleyways and dodged new dangers at every corner, pushing deeper into the maze of the unknown. The air grew thicker, the threat sharper. Every footfall, every clipped breath, counted. They had no powerful weapons—just grit and the stubborn refusal to stop. The sirens of the city hummed a wild chorus, ratcheting up the urgency. The mission now depended on one desperate truth: the chase had become their lifeline, and letting go meant losing everything.

When the pressure felt as if it might shatter them, a flicker of hope erupted. A rusty panel in the crumbling wall gave way to a dark pocket no one had counted on, inside flickering cold-blue drives stacked like bones. The moment the team of them pried them free, the weight of the find pressed on them: encrypted files that hummed with secrets they had dogged for months. A chill of recognition rippled—this was the last lock, the drop into the conspiracy's dark river. This was the final piece of evidence that could expose a high-level government conspiracy. With breath held and fingers shaky, they cracked open the first line of code, the screen's glow a fragile rearview mirror, reflecting the way toward the monsters they had promised to stop.

Tension dripped like rain off a crumbling roof as they huddled over the files, each open tab a fresh cut, revealing a network of misdirection that spread wider than the smokiest conspiracies. One by one, the documents fitted together, and the tasteful little map of intel on the screen shimmered with a cold, arithmetic clarity—pure radiation. Trust, once taken for granted like the office coffee, shrank until the next laugh in the break room felt treasonous. Every keystroke pulled the team a precarious step closer to the core of the chaos they had sworn to eradicate. That step felt like staring into fire. Yet, in the brittle-quiet room, a prophet star blinked: a path to parse, to dissect, to carve the rotten heart of the deception out. Iron-red courage snapped back to attention. They reset the filters, sorted the strings of lies like pearls from grit, and the room buzzed with the low hum of a gut feeling that this time, exposed the worm before the apple bit back. Collision now felt less like fear and more like a promise— and they urged the code forward as if the sunlight pushing through the blinds were the first blade of morning, cleaving the night.

In this high-stakes game of shadows, showing the truth would be their greatest victory, and with the ticking clock getting louder, the sprint to expose the dark scheme pushing the world toward ruin had only just begun. This was not just any scheme, but a meticulously planned and far-reaching plot that could plunge the world into chaos if not stopped in time.

As the timer steadily crawled toward zero, the air inside the room turned electric. Every member of the unit felt the knowing weight that the coming minutes would seal not only their mission but the safety of every corner of the globe. The data they had fished from the hidden underbelly of the server farm had guided their footsteps to this razor edge, and now the team stared down a fork that would echo through every decision to come.

Agent Thompson, rock-steady when everything else was flame, hung near the front of the line, eyes locked on screens whose glowing figures drummed the final countdown. Numbers never felt so alive—or so ready to kill. Thought after hurtling thought flashed through his mind, every possible play twisting on the pivot of risk and the slim chance of a bending reward.

Beside him, Dr. Invitation followed every number with the rhythm of a techno lullaby, lips pressed tight. Her speciality was mathematics, but tonight the only formula that mattered danced on the edges of the clock. She ran simulations the way others hum on long runs, eyes translating digits into outcomes—zero survivors, partial fail, complete world change—all untidy, all at hand.

Rodriguez crossed her arms on the table, her eyes scanning the screen again, her foot tapping the floor in a fast, nervous beat. Hours of code and firewalls had usually turned to clear red and green checkpoints for her, but this time, the light refused to confirm any path. Every fibre of her training screamed for expediency, yet the route ahead smelled faintly of irreversible harm. Across the table, Agent Reynolds traced the rim of his coffee cup, skin prickling with the flavour of his first real mission. The coffee had gone cold, same as his heartbeat whenever the readout flashed a mock countdown. He shot a fast glance at Embers and Ara, older eyes locked on the same blinking cursor. He borrowed the steadiness of their jaws to barricade his own doubts, even as the stakes of the following command rose like a slow tide. Then, as if the room had been shut in a cold room, Director Michaels spoke. He stood taller than the facts he carried and colder than the circuits in front of them. Each member of the team felt the hush in their chests, his black eyes lingering a beat, assessing, and then he said the one word that set the whole room spinning: decide.

The hush in the room felt almost like it was holding its breath, and they all felt the same chill—that one moment was about to become forever. Every single one of them sensed how deep the moment ran, how the choice they were about to make would ripple through time. So, without one word needed, they stepped forward together, their friendship and fight sharpened, ready to greet whatever storms their decision would unleash.

The instant the corridor of tension snapped, they entered the grey, shuttered room and found their enemy waiting. Dim light flickered against the stone, and the heaviness in the air pulsed louder than any heartbeat. Every member of the team could feel the test drawing tighter, the walls closing in like the last thread in a knot. Around them, doubt and courage tangled in the same breath. It felt like the hush itself was holding a flame, daring them to let it fight. Opposing gazes met across the dim space, unwavering. Each one bore scars of the past, a hunger for what was right, and the quiet promise never to step back.

Both of them understood this meeting would tilt the future, peeling back the messy layer of lies and treachery that had shadowed every step. In that charged heartbeat, silence roared with truths never spoken, armed with a certainty that would not bend, turning the room into a choreographed fight between sworn enemies—a clash not merely for power but for the spark of life in each of them.

Tension thickened like storm clouds; every sharp word struck like fire, peeling away the neat masks of calm that had kept fear, hurt, and doubt hidden. Every step, every syllable, carried the force of a loaded gun, a flirt with the edge of ruin. Inside that fierce deadlock, they knew only a single road could lead to forgiveness and survival; every other choice would hurl them into a dark finality they could not return from.

With every life in the room dangling by a breath, the final clash rolled toward its finish. A flood of iron will surged, and they stood before the moment that would define every heartbeat to come—a storm built from every victory, every wreck, and every burned dream. Here, the metal of their lives would strike together, and the reverberations of what they would choose would roll across time like thunder.

The blazing heat of the final moment promised either new beginnings, heavy changes, or ruin, testing the threads that hold life together. Every pulse sounded like marching feet, underscoring the steady advance toward the point that would decide where every shared path would go.

The room barely glowed, but the silence was bright with hope and dread. There, the chosen specialists from all the sciences faced a heavy fork in the road. Hollowed by long nights without sleep, the lines on their faces told of every doubt and every vow. Millions of lives dangled on a single breath, and that truth pressed down like great iron. Words hovered on the edge of every lip, yet no one spoke; each councillor tilted their minds, wading through the swirling sea of choices and fallout. The heights of danger soared above them, and room for mistake had vanished. Every path had been weighed, every ripple of consequence charted, yet still doubt occupied the corners of the room like a living guest. Dr. Catherine Marlowe, the one chosen to lead, lifted herself a fraction taller and faced them with a steadiness like stone.

Her voice carried a heavy weight that only years of service could put there. The room leaned forward, feeling her quiet strength. Sharp eyes found every corner and left no question unanswered.

"Listen. We stand at a turning point." The hush deepened as her words sliced through. "What we do now will ripple through history. We are at a crossroads, and the path ahead is uncharted and treacherous. Still, we must lead, to guide, and to stand for those who cannot stand for themselves."

The councillors, old and young, inclined their heads in solemn unity, faces set with the hard shine of purpose. They understood the weight of the choice before them, and none flinched.

"We must weigh every angle," Dr. Marlowe went on, her tone unyielding, "yet we cannot linger. The clock is against us, and a single pause could crumble everything. Please contemplate your beliefs, because the choice we make now will decide the future of whole nations."

Chapter Three

The Quantum Code

The team found themselves in a dangerous pinch when Croft's operators turned every corner into a firefight. Bullets hissed past their ears like angry hornets, and the ring of grenades turned the world into thunder. They had no heavy armour, no air support, and the street was a cage, but one thing the cage-masters never counted on was their brains. Within heartbeats, they schemed a plan, stacking their IQs taller than the city walls. Each corner they turned was a gamble, each shadow they crossed a dice roll, but they played the game like grandmasters. Numbers might be against them, but they weren't a maths problem; they were a story, and the story had more fight left. The team tightened the bonds that panic loosens, reading one another in a private, silent code. They guessed the enemy's next move the way a veteran gambler can smell a bluff and countered before the bluff was even spoken. Amid sirens and smoke, they remembered the stakes: if they fell here, the world-line might bend—and not for the better.

When the last fireball scorched the wreckage and the world caught its breath, Croft felt the ghost of the fight slide away. Then Nova's shadow slipped in behind it, a chill that wormed through every air vent and whispered in every lock. No alarms, no lights, just the balance of the last dice slipping into the dealer's palm.

When the team finished their hasty regroup and took stock of their weaknesses, Croft felt a bone-deep chill: Nova had engineered the perfect strike, and it had caught them cold. The cold discipline, the ruthless economy of force, spoke of a mind that saw every move three steps ahead, and that fact was a knife twisting in his gut. Out of the wreckage, though, Kofi had stepped up as an impossible hero. Steely under fire, he improvised a defence that sheltered the wounded and bought them minutes, maybe minutes that kept hope alive. Yet, the moment the true scope of Nova's hunger hit, it was clear they were no longer just responding to attacks; they were conducting a masterclass. Each peeled layer of Nova revealed a reach wider and a malice longer than Croft had dreamed, a spider's web whose centre crossed continents. Croft kept digging, translating the smeared chalk of sabotage and feints, and the nightmare crystallised: each sequence of provocation, every weak handle that had once looked trivial, had been memorised and hoarded for the kill, redrawing the terrain in Nova's colour. While he fought nausea, he felt the old burden change shape, no longer the cold tally of his team's flesh but the ledger of a planet. Nova's whisper was no longer a domestic disturbance, but the quiet before a storm that could drown cities.

Its tendrils slipped through every shield the old guards had ever raised, making defence a dying art. When he called the team together, Croft felt the weight of what lay ahead: an opponent whose cunning was a weapon sharper than any blade, whose manoeuvring could rewrite the fate of entire realms. The figure of Nova refused to be pinned—purpose wrapped in stillness. Yet as the fragments of the broader game drifted closer, a cold truth settled. Nova's design, its depth and width, was vast enough to drown continents. Each order, each quiet twitch, had already dropped a pebble that echoed towards empire-sized tsunamis. With every ticking second, the call to cut the rope holding Nova's knotted plan grew louder, more fevered. Threading the ever-shifting swamp of mirage and betrayal, resolve hardened inside Croft—pure, clear metal that could lend wings to weary hearts. Nova's latest sacrifice painted the long path of resolve that lay ahead, a pale ghost of their unbreakable resolve. Croft's team braced for the long night, the weight of every roof, every gathering storm, every pulse of every private child watchman now leaning squarely on their backs.

Kofi's heart pounded as he stepped from doubt into a storm of international conspiracy. The weight of every continent seemed to land squarely on his back. A lifelong diplomat, he had skimmed the surface of every political storm, but nothing had ever pressed so hard.

Inside the flickering halls of the United Nations, he found himself at the centre of a spinning web of lies. The peacekeeper inside him shouted to bring everyone to the table, but the table was tilting, and the price of failure was silence. Innocent lives balanced on a razor's edge, and the search for truth became the only voice he could hear.

Down the twisting corridors of power, he pried open secrets that turned polite banter into shrapnel. Hidden plans, long buried, clawed back into daylight, threatening to tear the globe apart. Even as the warnings grew louder and the risks grew personal, Kofi's will did not bend. Justice had chosen him, and he could not walk away.

Every fragile step forced him to stare at the choices diplomats usually dress in polite language.

The line between right and wrong had faded into a grey fog of shifting loyalties, and every night Kofi dreamed of surrender. Still, a single, stubborn spark of possibility refused to die. Armed with stubborn will and a mind honed like a blade, he dug at the mystery that had trapped nations, determined to become the lone candle flickering in a storm of lies. Anchored to the tattered creed of every mentor he had loved, Kofi set out on a road littered with jagged choices, each step a scalpel against the flesh of his own resolve. Every act towered like a dark cliff, decisions rippling outward, threatening to drown the future. Yet, with each new trial, a flame surged in his chest, stubborn and bright, urging him to march deeper into the chaos and fight. Kofi claimed the burden of leadership like a bitter oath, knowing the seeds he sowed today could grow into harvests of peace or blighted ruin. Steely honour locked his jaw as he crossed the threshold of ruin, ready to match truth against the night and become the voice future ages might still hear, naming evil by name.

The moment stretched like a wire ready to snap as Croft, weathered but still sharp, found a wall of gunfire closing around him.

The empty warehouse breathed gloom, its empty aisles full of shifting shadows and muffled gunfire thundering from the far end of its vast, cracked belly. Croft pressed his spine against the cold, corrugated face of a bent steel pillar, the bitter taste of fear and soot riding the back of his throat. Memory replayed years of drills, missions, and escapes; this was the tally slip for all of them. Croft edged his head half an inch into the blackness. A blur of grey scurried. He squeezed the trigger twice—two sharp chimes that cracked the dimness. The silhouettes ducked and cursed, but a heartbeat later the night twisted with more shadows, flooding out of half-seen doors and smoking vents. He felt the damp rope of dread across his shoulders, but slipped it away, letting the old, cool part of his mind take the wheel. He counted muzzle flashes, weighed cover, and calculated angles the way a sailor reads waves. A bullet hissed past his ear, searing the skin. Another, and another; each one a short, passionate whisper begging him to leave. The whisper roused something colder and harder inside him. Metal rang against metal like a giant's drum, and every thud was a warning, every burst of gunfire an echo of the last breath. Explosions popped like bitter fireworks, flaring the dusty air with red and grey. The warehouse felt alive, and Croft was its silent keeper, still resolute.

Through the chaos, Croft stood like a lighthouse, his eyes locked on the enemy's next move. Every muscle, every heartbeat, every drop of sweat poured into that fight, proving his will could not bend. When the weapons fell silent, a heavy hush rolled in, cold and deliberate. He stepped from the shattered wreck of the warehouse, his body a map of fresh and ancient wounds, and yet, he walked upright. The tale of his stand would ripple beyond those concrete walls, carving his name beside legends in the hush of a spy's memory. To

Croft, this was not a flash of violence, but the loud confession of a heart that would die before it sold out the living. A reminder, unmistakable and unpolished, that real courage is shaped, not born, in the furnace of cruel hours.

Cities sometimes listen, and that night, Paris was a confessional hush. News of Croft's stand raced through every back room and smoky tavern, a quicksilver warning and a silent promise that the night would crack open soon. Somewhere beyond the gilded bridges, a shadowed nook held a meeting as guarded as a secret tear, the sore of a city that knew it would soon bleed.

Kofi's new reluctant-hero life yanked him to the middle of a trap Nova built just for him, the dark puppet-master playing every string just right. Wandering the narrow streets, his shoulder blades prickled with the sense of some invisible eye nudging him along alleyways he wanted to forget. Each path he tested folded him back into the same slippery knot of danger. Streetlights flickered like nervous breaths, and somewhere behind him, a footfall mimicked every panic-stitch in his veins. Then the world folded in half. A form ghosted out of the kind of night that hides teeth, and in a beat, Kofi's heart stuttered to a frozen stop. The woman was nothing but a dark silhouette backed by secrets he barely understood. Her gaze—sharp and lighter than the street—finished the thought before he could speak: she was the sharper edge of the night. Kofi understood, and the understanding sliced like cold steel: he hadn't wandered here by accident. The piece was placed like a rook snuffing out a pawn, and he was the pawn going dark. Her footfall barely brushed the concrete, yet the sound filled the alley with a tight, choking night. The shadows seemed to lean in, and Kofi could almost hear the bricks giggling as they edged a little closer.

Every instinct inside him hummed like electricity. Kofi's mind swung between two choices: charge the shadow blocking the exit, or ghost past them like smoke. Seconds hung like slow poison as their gazes clashed, each searching for the crack where courage might give way to fear. Words stayed locked inside, the alley filled only with the weight of their moment. Kofi couldn't feel it yet, but the choices made here—under the flickering streetlight—were already bending the scales of a city on the edge. This silent contest was the first puzzle piece of a much larger game, a riddle of wits and heart that would sharpen into a confrontation neither would forget.

The moon balanced overhead like an unpolished coin, pouring ghost light onto the empty ground and asking questions the night did not try to answer. Silence pressed in, thicker than stone, and the empty space felt almost louder than during the fevered shouting in the halls above. Kofi, caught between the duty of a soldier and the whispers of a waking conscience, paused between the dully polished black columns. He was already far past the point of no return, yet the moonlight felt like a single compass needle that still pointed north.

They met in a half-lit alcove, far from council fires and guarded cheers. A form drifted in from the darker corner—properly dressed yet somehow unbound by cloth. The air seemed to thrum, the way old strings vibrate before a lute is touched. Kofi let his hand rest beside the guard's short hilt of his akimbo, not to menace, but to measure himself. Two pairs of eyes collided—his, a careful river; its, granite lake—and in that still, electric second, the world tightened its grip.

Neither spoke, yet the room pulsed with questions of loyalty, ambition, and the faces we offer mirrors. Kofi did not yet understand that this threadbare moment would unspool his settled beliefs and map a new continent of risk before the dawn.

It felt like thunder in close quarters: cultures colliding, dreams colliding, futures colliding—all magnetised toward the Quantum Code, glimmering like a distant star. During the tense debate, thinly veiled threats mingled with half-formed oaths, spinning a haze of doubt and fascination. Every utterance crackled with hidden agendas, revealing the ciphered charts of control and deceit that ruled their lives. For the first time, Kofi sensed the reach of unseen rulers, and he understood he was standing on the first rung of a stair that would swallow comfort, test every promise, and fracture the soul. The room thickened with the weight of impossible choices, the way the first drumbeat thickens the air before a storm. They finished, but gravity did not let them go; Kofi felt it tugging at the collar of his conscience, warning the calm underneath his skin. The next seconds, the next days, would unfold like futures no one had lived yet. In the silent alley outside, he tasted the iron of consequence on his tongue. He heard the low thrum of the first domino; he knew that the choices made here would not die on the plank floor, but would swirl through the wide sea of memory, bending lives and erasing edges of history.

The moment rewrote the rules beneath their feet, inviting them into a space where dreams thinned, and the Quantum Code waited to speak secrets the human mind could barely frame.

With every minute, the clock's steady breath sounded louder, and every member of Nova's crew felt the surge of history in their blood. They circled Pandora—the world's first true quantum lattice—as if it were a newborn sun. Dr. Kofi Anangwe, whose heart beat for questions nobody had dared to utter, stood unmoving, his gaze a laser through streams of recursive logic and braided qubit states. Silence sharpened to a knife's edge. Then a single, delicate note rang: the melody of the passkey unlocking the last gate. Faces lifted, and in those lifted faces gleamed the rare metal of victory. Before the celebration could take breath, an electric howl whipped through conduits. Lights dove, and the room drank night, yet their minds instantly rewrote the script. Power had not failed; power had changed. The calm of the room was shattered by a low hum that nudged the marrow, and from the heart of the lattice a pale, breathing light took shape, pulse for pulse, beneath the first quantum sky. In that radiance, every possible future stood watching.

The hush was ripped apart by a low, rising hum that rolled through the lab like the warning roll of distant thunder. It felt, to everyone in the room, as if Pandora herself was stirring after aeons of stillness. The scientists stared, hearts pounding in their throats, a fever of awe and dread. Then, unexpected, the noise vanished. Screens flared to life, brighter than the sun, bathing the lab in a cold, alien glow. Numbers, graphs, and swirling symbols erupted in a dizzying vapour of data that no human mind could comprehend all at once. Dr. Anangwe's voice cut through the dazzle, shaking and electric.

"We have—" he swallowed the wonder—"unleashed Pandora."

The words settled like lead pellets against the trembling walls. They understood, all of them, that Pandora could bend the very fabric of reality—that one config could rewrite the course of every factory, every hospital, every field. But a hunger for certainty could not tame a gift this vast. The team now stood at a seam, the fabric of time itself splitting, each stitch they now chose reverberating long after the lab doors closed. Their minds raced, calculations colliding with memories of ethics they had once thought safe. In that glowing, terrified hush, they knew they had stridden beyond the map, beyond experiment, into the quiet, boundless dark where knowledge and consequence were, for the first time, twins whose faces they could not name.

Pandora came loose, and a small fire lit that would grow into either a brilliant dawn or a dark ruin. What they had pulled free would ripple forward, bending the arc of history beyond the reach of any dream or dread.

The violence sang through the night like the voice of a restless god, and the city shivered. Neon signs shuddered, and the streets drank deep of shadow. Rival currents of ambition and creed pulled the same corner, and each man and woman felt the hum of an already-written letter that could be opened or sealed. Croft, the man too often re-membering sins he could not forgive, planted himself where road and river crossed. Bullets sang around him, sirens sang beneath him, and the heavy lump of what came next pressed like a hand in the small of the back. This was not a fight that nations would later dress in medals. This was a forge where private hearts and public destinies clashed and lit the air with sparks. Here, armoured machines remained cool-er than the thoughts that burned brighter than fire. While smoke-blurred faces shouted away a world, a young street preacher named Kofi stepped through the din like a candle through the dark.

Kofi stood beside Croft, the long, twisted road of his life leaving him here, just here, heartbeat and horizon. Every old wound throbbed awake; every whispered lesson from the departed pressed hard against his ribs. He met the dark, twisting force that wanted to bend the world's heartbeat into a weapon, and each gasp brought forward the strength he thought had leaked long ago. No sword drawn. No shouts. Just the quiet miracle of a man standing; just the stubborn belief that an ember can stare down a storm. This was his not to win; it was to meet, to settle the long quiet between flesh and mercy, to insist that the fragile, glorious pulse of human will, can still surprise the night.

Around them, the edges of reality rippled like half-remem-bered dreams. Tomorrow and yesterday clashed in a tan-gled blur. Whispers once called partners now walked in the mask of betrayal, every face smeared with the same oily lie. The quantum code—a shimmering riddle that, once solved, could stretch like a fist into every city and thought—hovered at their feet, humming with hungry quiet. At this jagged bend in time, Kofi and Croft, forged of light and grime, traded oaths with strangers and old reflections, knowing each syllable could drown or soothe a century. The world leaned forward, breath suspended, the fiery shape of what could be already clenching and unclenching in the bones of night. The only thing clearer than the dark was the song of the price: the cost of silence was now the cost of history.

It was here, inside a cyclone of thought and ambition, that everything—countries, lives, dreams—was about to change for good.

The air felt like charged wires when the two teams sat down, each mind polished to a razor's edge. Croft had always regarded himself as a master strategist. Still, across the polished table, Nova's squadron glowed with the same fierce honesty. The arguments, not rifles, would swing the balance. Every play was a scalpel, every choice a carefully forged key cutting toward three impossible locks that, once opened, could not be shut fast again. The hours folded like tight origami in the same breath, the ticking wall-clock a Kaplan coin landing the same face over and over. Probes of thought against a shield of thought, looking for the hairline fracture, the half-formed doubt. It was chess the size of continents, the board stretching into the tomorrow of everyone. Ideas forged in the furnace of doubt and quenched in question; rebuttals sparking like ferrocerium, yet the spark was the only bullet that could hurt.

This was no ordinary argument; it was a fight between the sharpest minds alive, the kind of duel where facts and theories served as our swords, and the strictest discipline of thought was the armour we wore. Whoever lost would not merely be embarrassed; their worldview would die. Inside the fortified chamber, conversation crackled like live wires. At the same time, a silent drumbeat of impatience quickened the pulse of the room. Leagues of ordinary people, strangers to the debate, stood as unseen witnesses; their futures hung in the balance, and retreat was unthinkable. And then, as if the clouds parted at last, a single pure idea rose like dawn, illuminating the hidden road no one had seen before. One argument pivoted, one strategy rerouted, and the conflict suddenly moved along a sharper, faster line. We both knew the battle had not ended, but a pale green shoot of tomorrow's success had been planted in the bedrock of pure thought.

Beneath the fading four hundred miles of tense silence, a single cold fact warned us all: the cost of inaction now dwarfed the cost of risk.

Against a sky bruised with unrest, Kofi and Nova were locked in a dangerous chess match where every piece shimmered with menace. The Quantum Code, a shimmering promise of either ruin or wonders, glimmered in the centre. The margin between salvation and ruin thinned to a razor edge, and Kofi felt its bite. Staring down a tide of fate, he threw himself into a maze of vanished whispers and sealed vaults, tracing a thread of lies until it pulled him to the pulsing core of Nova's design. All the while, Nova, her fingers tightening around the globe's pulse, breathed the last draft into her ruinous masterpiece, bending the core of quantum power to her cold, brilliant will. In the storm's eye, Croft, a man of bullet scars and iron guts, stood like a dark spire, his loyalty to a trembling order brighter than the storm. He had glimpsed the soot under every human soul. As the tide raced to a thundering peak, yesterday's vows were scored, fresh oaths born in hush, and the brittle thread of loyalty and betrayal snapped and rewove.

Bound by duty and fuelled by stubborn hope, Kofi rallied his friends, stitching together a brighter future even as darkness closed in. Together, they set out on a dangerous quest to undo Nova's ruthless plans, navigating a twisting maze of peril that lurked at every corner. The frantic dash toward the final hour led to a breathless showdown, where every ounce of light slammed against every ounce of shadow in a storm of courage and cunning. When the clock hit midnight, the Quantum Resolution detonated, brighter than any star. Sweat, strategy, and iron will, fused into a chorus of bravery and sacrifice, carving a narrow way to a second chance. When the smoke drifted away and the shock waves rolled around the planet, a fresh, golden dawn rose, bathing a world forever marked by the shudder of that moment.

Chapter Four

The Echoes of Meridian

The aftermath of Croft's defeat left a haunting echo that reverberated through the team and the global landscape. As the dust settled, their reflections intertwined with the shadows cast by the events that had unfolded. For the seasoned operatives of the clandestine unit, it was an opportunity to contemplate their roles in the grand scheme of this elaborate game of power and deception. Each member bore the weight of the recent crisis, examining every decision made and its consequential impact on their collective mission. The defeat of Croft was not merely the end of a battle; it was the awakening of a new reality.

As they gathered in the dimly lit conference room, the air seemed heavy with unanswered questions and unspoken fears. The implications of the fateful encounter rippled across the geopolitical landscape, casting a foreboding shadow over their intricate web of alliances and adversaries alike. The unsettling realisation dawned upon them that the aftermath of Croft's defeat would be felt far beyond their immediate circle. It was a domino effect, triggering a chain of repercussions that would shape the course of future operations and redefine the very essence of their endeavours.

Amidst the sombre atmosphere, the team members found themselves grappling with their vulnerabilities and doubts. The lines between friend and foe blurred as they navigated the murky waters of post-defeat introspection. Trust wavered, and suspicion lingered like a persistent spectre, heightening their awareness of the intricacies woven into the fabric of their enigmatic world. Each reflection was a testament to the fragility of their existence in the shadowy realm of covert manoeuvres. Beyond their isolated enclave, the global landscape bore the indelible marks of Croft's defeat.

The strategic equilibrium had been disrupted, ushering in an era of uncertainty and recalibration. Nations trembled at the implications of this seismic shift, recalibrating their agendas in response to the rearranged chessboard of power dynamics. The echoes of Meridian resonated through the corridors of influence, casting a poignant reminder of the vulnerability that lurked beneath the facade of supremacy. The aftermath was a grim tableau of shattered illusions and recalibrated ambitions, illuminating the inherent fragility of the prevailing order.

Following Croft's defeat, the team stood at a crossroads, teetering on the brink of uncharted territory. The shadows of the aftermath loomed large, shrouding their path with uncertainty. Each step forward carried the weight of profound introspection and unwavering resolve, for the echoes of Meridian had ushered in a new epoch defined by resilience in the face of adversity and illumination amidst the pervasive shadows.

The world was a powder keg, ready to ignite at the faintest spark. As chaos wreaked havoc across nations and shadows of turmoil grew longer, heroes found themselves caught in the crosshairs of an impending clash. Their identities concealed behind layers of duty and sacrifice, they stood as beacons of hope amidst the storm. Yet, within their hearts, a tempest raged, torn between devotion to ideals and the unyielding burden of responsibility. In the chambers of power, whispers circulated like ghostly apparitions, weaving a web of intrigue that threatened to entangle even the most valiant souls. The heroes, bound by oaths sworn in blood and valour, navigated treacherous waters, their every move scrutinised by unseen eyes. Each step they took bore the weight of countless lives. Yet, the harbingers of chaos remained insatiable, intent on shattering the fragile peace that still clung to the fraying edges of civilisation.

Amidst the labyrinthine corridors of influence, a clandestine adversary lurked, orchestrating a symphony of deception and manipulation. The heroes, stalwart and resolute, found themselves ensnared in a perilous dance of wits, pawns in a game where the stakes soared beyond measure. As adversaries closed in from all sides, the indomitable spirit of these champions flickered like a solitary flame in the encroaching darkness.

Unwavering in their resolve, the heroes delved deep into the heart of treachery, unravelling a tapestry of deceit that threatened to rend the fabric of their world asunder. Betrayal turned friend against friend, and the echoes of conflict reverberated through the hallowed halls of honour. In the crucible of adversity, bonds forged in the crucible of shared sacrifice emerged as the last bastions of hope, rallying against the inexorable tide of malevolence. As the dust settled and the maelstrom of chaos subsided, the heroes appeared, bearing scars that mirrored the collective wounds of a fractured world. Their spirits, tested beyond the limits of mortal endurance, burned with a newfound fervour, kindled in the crucible of adversity. Forged in the cauldron of uncertainty, they stood unwavering, a testament to the enduring resilience of the human spirit in the face of unfathomable tribulation.

The world trembled under the weight of its own contradictions. In every corner, the fractures widened, creating chasms that seemed insurmountable. Nations once allies now stood divided, their leaders entangled in a web of conflicting interests and shifting alliances. The geopolitical landscape had metamorphosed into an intricate mosaic of power struggles, where one wrong move could set off a chain reaction with unimaginable consequences. In the realm of technology, the divide deepened. Cutting-edge innovations became double-edged swords, blurring the line between progress and peril. As artificial intelligence advanced, so did the ethical dilemmas surrounding its applications. The race for dominance in cyberspace spawned clandestine operations, turning once benign platforms into battlefields for a virtual War with real-world implications. Trust eroded, and uncertainty loomed like an ominous cloud over the digital realm.

Meanwhile, the global economic order teetered on the brink of upheaval. Trade disputes escalated into full-blown economic warfare, as economic powerhouses clashed over tariffs and sanctions. Market volatility became the new norm as investors navigated treacherous waters fraught with unpredictability. The very foundations of international commerce strained under the weight of protectionism and financial brinksmanship, threatening to plunge the world into unprecedented chaos.   Societal divisions mirrored the fractures on the world stage. The fabric of communities unravelled amidst political polarisation and identity politics, sowing seeds of discord that threatened to tear societies apart.

Debates turned into battlegrounds, and compromise became a relic of a bygone era. Trust in traditional institutions wavered, as populism and extremism gained traction, tugging at the seams of democracy itself.   Amidst this turmoil, whispers of hope emerged from the shadows. Movements advocating for unity and understanding kindled flickers of resilience in the face of adversity. Innovators and visionaries sought to harness the power of technology for the greater good, envisioning a future where advancements served as a beacon of progress rather than a harbinger of discord. Voices from across the spectrum called for dialogue and reconciliation, daring to dream of a world mended rather than shattered. A fractured world stood at a crossroads, poised between dissolution and transformation. The choices made in the crucible of uncertainty would shape the destiny of nations and individuals alike, determining whether the echoes of division would reverberate into oblivion or converge into the symphony of a new era.

The world stood at a perilous juncture, teetering on the edge of chaos and possibility. As the echoes of Meridian reverberated through the corridors of power and reverent institutions, nations found themselves at a crossroads - a convergence of divergent paths that would shape the very fabric of history. The geopolitical landscape resembled an intricate chessboard, with each move carrying grave consequences. Levers of influence and subterfuge were being pulled in shadowy chambers and clandestine enclaves, fuelling the flames of uncertainty and distrust.

Amid this turbulent tempest, individuals of unparalleled resolve found their mettle tested. Agents of clandestine organisations embarked on treacherous missions, navigating a labyrinth of deceit and danger, driven by allegiance to cryptic causes and unwavering patriotism. Their actions became the nexus upon which fate pivoted, for they held the keys to unlock the shackles of impending devastation or herald an era of unforeseen prosperity.

Meanwhile, world leaders grappled with the weight of momentous decisions, their choices echoing through the annals of time. The sanctity of alliances hung in precarious balance, as the spectre of conflict loomed on the horizon. A whisper could tip the scales, inciting unrelenting clashes and unleashing the dogs of war. The world watched with bated breath, cognizant that the tides of destiny were inexorably intertwined with the decisions made in these crucial moments.

At the heart of this global conundrum lay the interplay of ideology and ambition, entwined in a dance as ancient as civilisation itself. In boardrooms and war rooms, strategic minds devised intricate plans and countermeasures. At the same time, the pulse of espionage and intelligence quickened with every heartbeat. Yet amidst the intricate web of political machinations and covert operations, a glimmer of hope shone through. It was the realisation that at the precipice of discord, the potential for unity and reconciliation flickered like a luminous beacon, offering a path towards harmony and cooperation. The crossroads of destiny beckoned, casting its long shadows over the world stage. For as the players of this grand theatre pondered their next moves, the weight of history bore down upon them, demanding that they tread cautiously yet decisively on the path forward.

The spectres of conflict loomed like dark clouds on the horizon, casting ominous shadows over the war-torn landscape. The echoes of battle reverberated through the air, a haunting symphony of violence and chaos. In the aftermath of the recent clashes, the once bustling streets were now deserted, their silence a painful reminder of the toll of war. Scattered debris and broken remnants bore witness to the ferocity of the struggle that had unfolded. Amidst the devastation, whispers of defiance and resilience lingered, refusing to be drowned out by the cacophony of destruction. The indomitable spirit of the survivors permeated the atmosphere, a testament to the unyielding human will in the face of adversity. Yet, amidst this resolve, uncertainty hung heavy in the air, its weight felt by all who dared to dream of peace. Within the heart of the conflict, disparate factions clashed with fervour and desperation, each driven by their own motivations and agendas. Lines blurred and alliances splintered, giving rise to a maelstrom of shifting loyalties and clandestine machinations. At the centre of it all, a pivotal struggle for power and control raged on, its outcome poised to shape the destiny of nations.

As the spectres of conflict continued to cast their long shadow, strategic minds grappled with difficult choices and calculated risks. The fog of war enveloped the battlefield, obscuring the distinction between friend and foe. Every step forward was fraught with peril, every decision a gamble with uncertain consequences. Amidst this crucible of chaos, leaders emerged, their mettle tested and their resolve unwavering in the face of insurmountable odds. Yet, amidst the turmoil, flickers of hope ignited in the darkness. A whisper of unity, a glimmer of understanding, hinted at the possibility of reconciliation. It was in this crucible of conflict that the true nature of humanity was laid bare, its capacity for both unspeakable cruelty and boundless compassion on full display. As the spectres of conflict continued their dance across the ravaged landscape, they unwittingly set the stage for a new chapter in the age-old saga of war and peace.

After the last echoes of gunfire faded, the map of nations bore scars no treaty could erase. Nations stood stunned, facing the hollow chill of what they had done, the choices of yesterday refusing to vanish. Yet, amidst the silence of decaying battlefields, an unanticipated flicker caught the eye: the quiet arrival of redemption.

When the smoke finally lifted, men and women of every kind found themselves standing at the same fork. Soldiers, faces lined with unspoken regrets, wanted more than medals; they wanted to replace the pain they had spread. Neighbours who once watched swap rumours now moved arms, food, and courage, proving that everyday hearts could hold what now felt impossible. These separate roads, each heavy with memory, met at a single urgent, unanswered question: how do you heal a world that feels unhealable?

Leaders took a breath, and the map folded again: friendships re-drew, colours changed. Old beliefs met new truths at the conference table and at the cracked edge of a village. Those small, unsure choices made in the edge-light of night would be the ink that wrote tomorrow. Within that fragile light, the face of redemption stood clear: more than forgiveness, it was the quiet willingness to listen until yesterday's enemy spoke the same quiet shame, and to walk a new kind of future together.

When the world felt like it was coming apart, a few brave hearts stepped up, daring to steer the ship of world relations even through the roughest seas. They somehow infused the winds of the world's edges with a fresh, hopeful music that hummed of solidarity and grit. With tired but steady hands, they spun a careful dance of treaties, hush-hush talks, and patient compromise. At the core of this slow, burning recovery stood the human heart, refusing to break or scatter. It crossed walls and rival flags, tying strangers into one long, shared wish for a kinder day. Steel collided and voices thundered, yet somehow talk overcame gunfire, and hands once drawn into fists began to lift one another. This was proof that change lives inside all of us, that from the embers of anger, something like forgiveness and fresh starts can bloom. The road ahead is still shadowed and twisting, but it shines here and there with hints of healing and new life.

As the world balanced on the edge of unstoppable change, the flame of redemption blazed bright, guiding the way to a tomorrow not chained to yesterday's wounds, but open to the gold of a fresh sunrise.

Within full-throated turbulence, a daring pivot was born, a delicate reel of strength and stealth choreographed for the battles to come. In government offices lit by flickering screens, partnerships crackled like dry brush, ancient trusts cracking beneath the weight of new, wrenching decisions. Every nation paused, every heartbeat measured against stories already written and dreams unwrapped, for this gamble promised everything. The chessboard was molten, and the pieces knew it. Then the taller shadow known only as the Architect flickered into view, composing discord into a low, terrible music only the powerful could hear. The Architect hid behind a glare of silence, but continents moved at the brush of that hand, borders softened and siege lines drawn by email, by night, by hush. Undercurrents of masked rendezvous and coded air freight whispered chill through embassies and barracks, while the Architect's reach curled around cabinets and command desks like the night folding bay.

Across the front lines, commanders wrestled with the never-ending churn of agreements broken and renewed. Divisions crossed borders, robots and tactics learning together, while the balance of power hung like a thin stream of water. Every order felt like it carried a planet's future, every skirmish a step along the knife's cutting edge. In that storm, one small figure moved quietly, feeling every hidden current and carrying the ache of choices still unborn. Agents, half-seen witnesses of twilight, glided through the threads of spies and sabotage, their oaths wavering as the chill of future treason whispered. Nations peered into the dawn, searching for the first flash that would summon the giants, when rumours of a secret meeting suddenly lit the shadow. Minds gathering, decisions that would cast shadows over the lives of millions. In that sealed chamber, every breath carried the weight of centuries. The grand turn was nearly upon them, a single point of intersection where every wavering strand of coincidence, courage, and regret would braid together into fire or treaty.

Around the world, leaders, generals, and analysts steeled themselves for the shock wave they sensed trembling just out of view—an echo of past ruins and present choices. Picking tomorrow in the velvet-trimmed chamber, the heads of state formed a semicircle, the polished table a battlefield of polished faces. Jawlines tightened; fingers drummed; polished shoes remained anchored on the floor, refusing the tug of old quarters or old grudges. A hush louder than an oncoming storm pressed against the gold-leaf ceiling. Every continuity or break in the chain of command was written in the silence. Walls of microphones hummed with the electricity of unspoken pacts, the languages of leverage and loyalty. Outlines of treaties flashed beside whispers of covert programmes; past treaties—half-kept—lay mouldering in the corner. Tempers flared in coded and public tongues, and the glare of screens caught unshed tears in the eyes of those who knew the price of failure. Yet somewhere in the tangle of elbows and alliances, a calm, collective breath ordered the tempest. Draft statements drifted out like flares, illuminating paths both familiar and foreign. Hour after hour, the argument crashed against old rocks, then found a new, unsteady shore.

Each person in the room felt the weight of leadership pressing down harder with every spoken word, every silence longer because they all knew the choices they made today would ripple into tomorrow, shaping a future still hidden from them. Doubts flickered like candle flames in their eyes, lighting the furrows on their brows, but never quite quitting the dark. Plans hung, trembling, between daring advance and careful pause, and in every moment the thin line between clever move and moral breach was redrawn on the living board of fate. A fragile agreement began to crystallise, hammered from hours of fierce argument and tempered by the cold truth of the greater common good. Each person, loyal to their own country, nonetheless reached for the piece of ground where all could stand. Give-and-take, whispered oaths, scrawled treaties—each name signed was a promise and a burden, the weight of nations and quiet families pressed into ink.

Through the charged air, a quiet, iron resolve swept like a chill wind. Whoever later opened the records would feel the imprint of this hour. Schemes still pulsed beneath the calm, but they were calmed, weighed, and for the moment held still by sheer will. The uneasy dance between hunger for victory and the fear of ruin, balanced on a thread so thin it might snap or shine.

When the last words were spoken, a stillness folded over the room, thicker than smoke. Roads had been chosen, kismet braided where it had once been loose. The door that opened—straight, narrow, and unknown—carried the shared, quiet promise that they would walk into the waiting dark, together.

Troubling shadows, some visible, others just whispers, now gathered far beyond the sunset, folded in silence, ready to braid their fate into the days to come. The gamble had been sealed, and the shared vow still rumbled through marble hallways, clanging like cautious bells above an unknown tomorrow.

The air was alive with crackling tension as rulers from distant lands faced one another as wary players in a game that could jump off the board. Within smoke-draped chambers, their thoughts tangled into smoky spirals of advance and retreat, each idea walking a razor line between fire and pause. Over the mapping of the globe, the shadow of war spread its dark wings, and the far rumble of thunder—perhaps cannon, perhaps storms—shuddered through the halls. Wordy bridges of diplomacy had turned to frost, and the silence was broken only by short, cold letters signed with frostbite. Each morning, the board changed colour, pieces moving into tighter, bleaker shapes, locked in a waltz between command and surrender. At the core of this woven night of secrets and strength, the clash of minds beat like distant war drums, steady, unyielding, and loud enough to drown the songs of civilians waiting for midnight.

Dark clouds gathered, and the titans of government fought, their drives and certainties colliding in a brutal, beautiful din. Behind the courteous language of treaties, animal instincts stirred, each capital clutching its secrets and its must-haves with cold fingers. The fragile spine of power—fashioned through years of whispered bargains and bitter bargaining—now swayed like a fraying thread, bound to snap and rip the fragile cloth of peace. The ticking clock, indifferent to the frightened hush, marched closer to a horizon none could name, and the shadow of war darkened every capital. In the still, shadowed chambers, the shapers of fate felt the world's memory pressing on their backs, every notation a brick of choice and dread. The mental and the metal collided in a furnace of bitter strategy, where entire futures dangled like threadbare rafters, and a single wrong step could send the floor tumbling under a continent. In that pulsing black centre, the clang and clash sharpened again, hammering both wills and alliances under the strain.

Behind the flowery speeches and careful gestures, the real face of power peeked through, showing the raw ache of human desire and the cold laws of world politics. The voices of earlier wars echoed in the corners of every debating hall, a ghostly drum reminding all the stubborn leftovers of fighting and how thin peace really is. In the furnace where ideas collide with steel, everyone quieted, balancing on the knife-edge of what tomorrow would remember. Each sentence, each order, weighed more than those who spoke it could imagine, bending the fates of whole countries and the larger arc of human travel. As the last pieces were moved on the immense board of world diplomacy, the ghost of the Meridian period passed like a pale tide, stitching itself, forever visible, into the book of who we have always been.

When the smoke of the last confrontations cleared, an almost electric hush wrapped the globe. Everything shimmered with possible futures, each breath a small tilt toward one. Survivors of the fighting, the new map of power was still wet with doubt, and the old borders of friendship and betrayal were redrawn in real time.

Leaders tracked every move across the global chessboard, plotting futures behind velvet curtains while invisible agents skirmished in the half-light, striking foes the world would never know. But in that swirling dark, a few steadfast souls burned like lighthouse fires, pushing through doubt with the force of their iron wills. Powered by unbendable morals and quiet certainties, they redefined what bravery means when the walls close in. Out of that fire, a faint road began to reveal itself. When the last guns cooled and silence settled like ash, the hour of stillness arrived. Every side, every key player, was forced to ask the same probing question: what now? The reply would never come from maps or battle plans alone; it would arise from a bone-deep reexamination of why they fought, what they yearned for, and which dreams had carried them toward different horizons. Beneath the surface of every leader, a stubborn flame burned to write a different story, to steer toward a promise that old skirmishes could never limit. The future stretched ahead, veiled and trembling, but radiating with unshed light.

The path ahead was littered with danger and steeped in sacrifices so large they were hard to even imagine. Still, it dangled the sweet promise of breaking the chain of endless conflict and pain. From the wreckage of the old system, a new vision flashed like a bright bird, eager to lift itself against a world that was tired of fighting and longed for peace. The moment of choice had come, and every person, tucked safely in their own world yet feeling the pull of the crowd, weighed the hard choices that hovered before them. At this point, moving forward was more than just walking some road; it was a deep turn in how power and respect between nations—and how we all treat one another—would be imagined from now on. This moment would ask for costs we had yet to calculate, it would test friendships, and it would rise up against beliefs we had held the longest. Yet buried in that test was the strange, bright force we call hope, along with the promise that we could start again, cleaner and wiser. So the first light of this new chapter glimmered over the ground we were to tread, the curtains of time were drawn, and the saga that would one day be told again and again was ready to begin, its glow already tracing bright lines across the future we were still dreaming.

Chapter Five

THE NEW DAWN

The Meridian Protocol has stripped away the facade protecting every country's most fragile points and shown that only radical, immediate change will prevent the world from descending into even worse chaos. When the Meridian Syndicate's dark campaign concluded, the loud silence that followed was the shock of realisation. The intricate lattice that keeps our lives, our economies, and our safety interconnected was laid bare, wire by wire. The net we once thought of as weightless and private now appeared cruelly tethered to the physical world, where switches, pipes, and heartbeats could be manipulated by distant hands.

Officials moved faster than their own alarms could sound, racing to quantify the wounds the Syndicate had inflicted. Power grids, blockchains, subway systems, defence lines—each once-invisible seam now glimmered with fracture. The structure we had dressed with confidence was sagging, barely held together by a pallid thread. Shock melted into the bright heat of orders and meetings, for every leader recognised that isolation was now a fatal luxury. The strange candour that a nation's borders could not shield from a storm of this magnitude forged a fragile camaraderie. Old enemies, bored rivals, and lapsed allies now spoke the same language of repair and mutual protection, their ancient grievances muted by the same cold, shared fear.

Even as the new dawn illuminated the horizon, faint whispers of doubt clung to the high halls of power. How could nations truly unite when every corner harboured mistrust? The person-to-person bond that made partnerships thrive lay in ruins after the Meridian shock. Now, in the ruins, every capital tallied the cost and the gift of collaboration, nervously measuring the thin line between standing alone and standing together. The shadow of retribution still stretched long; in a world where loyalties shifted at the first gunshot, mercy felt more like a fable than a choice. Spies and shadow-messengers still spun half-truths and echoes, clouding every goal and bending every heart to a purpose that might not be their own. Circles of doubt spun faster than circles of action, and the hard-won dawn that once promised shared bright days began to waver under the weight of forgotten trust.

Then, from quiet corners, voices rose that few had anticipated. Professors, start-up dreamers, street campaigners, and village storytellers asserted that nations were stitched together not only by shared fear, but by the shared dream of what could be.

Diplomats, in long-pressed bow ties and silent suits, stepped toward each other, searching for bridges over centuries-old wounds. Yet with every clasped hand and cautious smile, the unspoken fear loomed large: Would the storm of fresh words build a shared shield, or crack apart beneath the weight of yesterday's grudges?

The drumbeat of war still rattled the maps on oak walls, leaving shredded treaties and frayed eyebrows. Yet from the wreckage a thin, shimmering promise spread: allies remade. Former enemies now squinted at the same silhouette that loomed at the edge of every courtyard. This nameless circle reached into the cracks of the world. As rumours of daggers flew from capital to capital, envoys in seamed overcoats met in dark train stations and dim cafés, sifting for words hot enough to melt old iron. Grudges that had forged treaties for lifetimes shimmered and then, with a gasp of cold air, settled into tide pools of cautious strategy. In the hushed halls where a misplaced comma could sway battalions, scar tissue was painted over with the thinnest coat of paint called "urgency." They sketched a bargain: a guardrail, not a handshake, designed to hold until the next calm or the next storm.

Doubt still smeared the polish of this odd friendship. Still, the common dread of impending extinction fused old enemies in a shaky agreement. Spies on every shore and continent reached over the spikes of old mistrust. Secrets once prized and locked away were now slipped in coded whispers, every scrap of knowledge a fragile strand in the huge net of lies they all sought to tear apart. Balancing on the narrow line of treaties and shadows, untried battlefields sprang to life–partnerships built on cold need, not the warm glow of confession. Men who shape the world's game watched like surgeons over a tingling incision, aware that cooperation pressed together by fear always risks explosion. Still, in the furnace of doubt, tired alliances were reheated, the metal of treaties growing seared and stronger. The planet held its breath as old enemies stepped into tomorrow's shade, pushed by the same hunger to stay alive. Hatreds that had burned for a thousand years were shoved into the same narrow cell, and the bars were being rattled. How long they would hold—or bend—none yet knew over the low rumble of the coming dark. As night fell on the maps, the echoes of new loyalties shook the world as loudly as a locked door swinging wide.

The fires of discord had melted old loyalties. From that red-hot chaos, fragile new bonds began to take shape, faint yet shimmering—tiny beacons in a storm that refused to relent. Now, in that uproarious twilight, friend and enemy shuffled so closely together that only the thinnest thread of fragile balance kept the carnage at bay.

The Crossroads of Destiny lay veiled beneath a tangle of forbidden jungle, a hidden scar on the world map that only whispered legends had ever marked. Here, on the moss-slick stone that felt both altar and executioner, the fortunes of mighty realms dangled like a single spark on a razor's blade. Inside the moss-stained clearing, history cracked its knuckles, and the air scored itself with nerve and sulphur. Delegates from every corner of the globe stepped from the shadows, their masks of diplomacy thin enough to let fear shine through. Rumours of knives planted in backs and contracts signed in darkness dogged their every word, and the jungle bent its ears to listen.

They settled around a table of black stone, veins of crimson thread pulsing like captured blood. Delegates squared shoulders decorated with every star and stripe, yet felt the same hollow in the chest that pulsed in every hungry village. Silence expanded, and inside it the future began to tremble. Every speaker's tongue carried the weight of a million live souls, and every decision made in that tangled clearing would be folded into the pages that gods, historians, and the children to come would one day read.

The Crossroads of Destiny had become a dangerous stage where diplomats exchanged polite words while others wove deadly lies. From the first moment the talks opened, it was clear that old grudges and secret plans were ready to blow apart any hope of agreement. Voices rose louder than reason; fingers pointed, accusations turned to fists. Just when it seemed the argument would swallow them all, a piece of truth sliced through the noise, revealing a dark and hidden group moving between the dark corners of the world. They called themselves the Unseen Adversary. Whispers of this secret power rippled through every delegation, forcing kings and rebels alike to think again about who their friends really were. The Unseen Adversary had spun a net of lies so fine that the sharpest eyes had missed it, and now the whole world hung by a single thread. The delegates, trembling and fierce, faced the crossroads with their true selves laid bare. They had to choose, and the moment would decide not just their own futures, but the futures of every city and tribe that breathed under the same sky. Reason and treachery fought like fire and flood, and every word spoken seemed to glow with the weight of a thousand swords. Here, at this hardened crossroads, the fates of nations were braided like steel, and every leader who dared to speak now turned the wheel of destiny.

The night pressed down like a heavy cloak, smothering the city in a deep and cold silence. Streetlamps flickered, weak and uncertain, their light swallowed by the thick darkness that seemed to pulse with hidden eyes. Muffled footsteps echoed like quiet thunder, and the walls themselves seemed to lean in, listening. From rooftop to cellar, the air tasted of warning, and every unlocked door felt like an invitation to something that should stay far away. In a cellar council of the forgotten, a single figure, shrouded, unveiled a token—no more than a dark, broken seal—and the room held its breath. The mark was known to only a few, yet it spoke of betrayals old and rituals never forgone. Outside in the chill, shadows waited, and the night itself held its breath, poised between the dead past and a trembling dawn.

Under sickly orange streetlights, a small crew swept through the night, moving like smoke and leaving no whisper behind. Somewhere among them, a hidden hand turned the world with careful fingers, and even the sharpest eyes could only guess. The city seemed to breathe a colder air, like a pulse drawn back, while half-formed rumours slipped from mouth-to-mouth, stitching a blanket of dread across the quiet. Secret meetings trembled between the brick canyons, their footsteps melting like frost, and the city itself felt the sting of betrayal sewn into every sigh. The architects of disorder moved with clockwork calm, leaving no telltale signs, while they laced the streets with false light and false hope.

Somewhere, still, our unwilling heroes stood on blurred lines between hunted and hunters, marionettes tugged by strings finer than dust, and wondering if they could ever snap the puppet master's grip. Each new alley, each damp corner, drove them nearer the centre. At the same time, the enemy melted again, identity still smeared like smoke in a doorway. They plunged deeper, the heat of hidden rooms and ruined minds burning the night, and one by one the rotten truths unreeled—it was not a city-wide conspiracy, not a crooked hand in a single pocket, no, it was a net that draped across oceans. This betrayal had already engraved its first letters far from the street they stood on.

Dread settled thick around them, urging our heroes to look the monster in the eye that prowled their every breath. The truths that surfaced felt like knives: the futures of entire nations dangled over a dark drop, yanked by a force too huge to name. When the last shard of the charred puzzle slid into view, a cold, clear knowing spread—against them loomed a foe whose strength shattered the limits of what the living could grasp. Still, out of that choking dark, a thin, fierce light flared, kindling a stubborn fire in the chests of those brave enough to meet the invisible storm. Linked by a cause that left no room for retreat, they wove a bond of steel—an oath to face the rise of a dark tide that hungered for everything they loved. Their defiance blazed like a quicksilver star, guiding the way through a sea of blacker nights. When the last black chill receded and haunted dawn kissed the rooftops, the heroes stood on the last lip of safety, poised for the clash that would carve the coming years into victory or ruin.

The hidden enemy had lurked in darkness for long enough; the moment had arrived to drag it into the light and shatter the plots that meant to drown the world in unrest.

The alliance felt the bad news like a cold wind cutting through every capital. The Unseen Adversary had woven a slow, silent assault, tugging the threads of every treaty and border with a calm that froze the blood. Once the truth broke, emergency councils across hemispheres snapped into motion. Spectres of past decisions rose before every statesman, whispers of choices made and ignored, now returned, teeth bared, ready to gnaw through the present. Beneath the chill blue glow of secure rooms, forgotten accords and concealed designs flashed into the open, stared into one another, and coalesced into a shaky treaty whose only bond was the fear of collective extinction. Hours bled into mournful days. Former rivals—sacrificing their histories like worn boots—stepped into the same boat. Old distrust rotted the hull. Old betrayals peppered the air. Yet, every gaze fixed on the horizon, where the shadow still lurked, tightening its grip.

Yet in the middle of the storm, a quiet spark of light started to glow—an unspoken agreement settling like a quiet promise among them: to face the approaching evil, they must walk the road of shared healing together. Old sins hovered like mist above the gathered leaders, reminding them in grim whispers that only by admitting their deeds and seeking to right them could they stand shoulder to shoulder against the coming dark. Inside the heat of torn loyalties and splintered treaties, astonishing new friendships took shape, and grudges that had festered for years were buried for a cause far grander than revenge. For certain among them, the trek down Atonement's Path felt like climbing a mountain of fire, demanding introspection and the kind of drop-your-guard humility that rarely arrives uninvited. Scars long ago closed ripped open again, and feelings long buried surged up, for the dawning truth of their common weakness finally sank in, pushing them toward a shared judgment of their own hearts. Every partner in this choice-torn fellowship dragged the chain of their own regrets, wrestling memories of the choices that had let this dark tide roll in. Yet, though the mountains of danger still towered above them, a cautious blossom of togetherness began to creep among the weary, mismatched ranks.

Friendship and respect began to bloom among us because we all wanted to change and make peace with what we had once broken. Determination lit a spark in our hearts that turned into a flame we swore never to let die. We promised ourselves we would make right what had once gone so very wrong, and we would guard tomorrow so that the darkness could never again creep into life. Along the winding Atonement's Path, the toughest trial still loomed, waiting patiently.

It would ask the deepest kind of giving and the strongest kind of togetherness, especially when the enemy matched our fierce drive with its chilling trickery.

The air crackled with electricity as rival operatives circled the table, fists clenched, lips pressed tight. Every watch ticked like a judge's gavel. Months of skirmishes—silent taps on undersea cables, hushed corridors, the fleeting flash of a forgotten password—had led them to this room. Now, with the final seconds of a crucial negotiation bleeding away, the balance of power dangled above the abyss. One move, one whisper, one slip, and the world tilted.

Across the scarred wood, the board glittered like a galaxy of moths. Every tile shimmered with fractals of friendship and fracture. Old vows, new debts, double agents reciting the wrong nursery rhyme. Everyone at the table knew: what unfolded here wouldn't spoil like milk. It would burn its way through continents, reshaping borders, currencies, and children's names.

Yet above the hushed buzz of microphones, the real game danced and shimmered somewhere else. Two masked silhouettes, faces shrouded by shadows and intentions, traded invisible daggers, sharp as the sting of betrayal, across the half-lit arena. Blue eyes. Steel-grey eyes. One blinked; the other narrowed. Each pulse, each breath, bled into a shape only the fates could read.

Behind the calm masks they wore, something wild stirred, pushed by old grudges, hidden vows, and the never-ending chase of their own plans. Still, even in the rising anger, a thin streak of respect flashed, a quiet echo of their shared past that kept them circling in this dangerous duel of minds and hearts. Round by round, the scales of power drooped like a tightrope about to snap, the room thrummed with the buzz of a truth about to drop. Hushed hints of secret missions and hidden plays slithered through the air, a cold reminder of the dark seam that lay beneath the polished talk and polished suits. Here, in this realm of shadows and silk, the space between friend and enemy grew thin, and pacts were made and broken in a heartbeat. With every second, the arc of destiny tipped and tipped again, moving toward a drop that could not be retraced. The burden of the coming choice pressed hard on every seat, each mind wrestling with what their hand would write and the fog of what lay beyond. When the bell of that moment finally tolled, tension climbed the last rung, a quiet roar rising to the hush before the fall.

As the last pieces of the grand chessboard slipped quietly into rank, one truth rose like the first light of dawn: everything was about to change. The powers that had carved the wheel of the world for generations now stood ripe for overturning. The balance of might, once a stone that would never move, trembled. Ahead lay a rupture unlike any ever recorded, one that promised a fresh map of influence, with new alliances and enmities, and a whole new set of rules for the game, as the first pale gleam of a changed age lifted into view.

The air was a curtain of electricity; you could taste the coming storm upon your tongue. Candlelight flickered in the vault, casting moving shadows across the tired faces of the councillors, who sat in taut silence, shoulders hunched beneath the weight of tomorrow. Each was aware, in their bones, that the judgment about to fall from their lips would etch the contour of earth and sky. Such a truth deepened the stillness to a grave hush. The odds climbed higher than any wager of their forebears; the ripples of their choice rose like a black wave. Nations, perhaps oceans of humanity, balanced on the brittle edge of that single word. It was a burden vast as night, and fewer still than the room could count had the fortitude to carry it.

There was no room for pausing or second-guessing—the clock struck the hour, calling for fearless choices. While the council huddled, voices crashed against one another, furious athletes in the arena of thought. Every member hurled forth their argument, passion shimmering in their eyes, their words crashing against the stone walls like wild waves against the cliffs of what was yet to be. It became a gladiatorial contest of beliefs, a storm of dreams that nearly tore the circle apart as battered banners of opposing plans tore through the crowded hall. Then, from the boiling din, one voice sliced the noise like sunlight through a thunderhead. It was steady, cool with the fire of long years, and every ear turned to the utterance. Its syllables carried the weight of old learning and clear sight, sketching a narrow, ringing pathway out of the whirlwind that sought to swallow their every hope. Minutes thinned to spilt sand as the council tugged against the choice that hung above them like the last storm of winter. Candle flames flicked and bowed, throwing trembling lights over the aged brows of the council, and every crease on their fierce faces shone like iron under the strike of a hammer, locked on a single purpose.

The weariness tugged at their bones, yet not one among them allowed even a shrug to show. At last, when pale dawn crept through the chipped glass, a hush like held breath crept over the hall. That hush was heavy, weighing every word yet to be spoken, every choice yet to be claimed. Inside that hush, the leaders quietly, without a feather of doubt, agreed at last. This verdict, hammered from every argument, tempered in fires of conscience, quietly set the wheels of the empire in motion. Its echo climbed the marble stairs, stirring courtiers and counting ink that would never be unwritten. Sheeting them was the certainty that the storm would howl against the door, and still, their backs locked straight. The pieces had moved; the stage had flickered to life; soon the empire would be shaped by the shape of a single, breath-held choice.

In every heart of that wide chamber, a drumbeat of hope and dread held tempo. Two visions, each burning with stolen loyalty, stood shoulder to shoulder like twin swords at dawn. Nations leaned forward, their lifeblood held in the delicate cup of time, balanced above the yawning dark.

Every breath felt heavy with years gone by, hanging in a tight pause before the storm. On one side stood a line of faces carved from honour and custom, every glance a promise to defend the old flag; on the other, restless hearts coursed with the heat of a world yet to be born, arms outstretched toward the bright unknown. Their stares, few yet burning, clashed in silence, each side waiting to lay down body and soul for a story only half of them could write. Diplomacy, patched with a fragile thread, thinned until one syllable, one twitch, even the wrong length of breath, split it like ice on a lake. In that narrow space, the voices of every long fight drifted like ghosts, loading every syllable with the weight of treaties broken and first embassies built. The old feuds and the new friendships met and swirled, the fruit of years of secret maps and hidden letters, and the tall, quiet measure of the room turned into a choreography only the blind could hear: the last step leading to a bow, or to the first roar of guns. Energy hummed in the dust, a storm of fear and pride and hope brushing the careful masks the leaders plastered on.

The weight of old wounds felt like a storm cloud, low and heavy, ready to snuff out the tiny, new flame of hope that had unexpectedly flared. But just on the edge of that thick grey, a brief, quiet sparkle suggested that an answer, not yet clear, might still be waiting a heartbeat away. Everyone knew the cost of failure, too vivid to ignore, and that terrible edge loomed sharper with each slow inhale. Yet, each person in the room balanced on the narrow strip between deliverance and disaster. Inside the fire, paths twisted like vines knotted in motion, each choice vibrating with the wild, uncertain truth of what it means to be human and the stubborn fire that will not go out.

When the final echoes of the battle faded like thunder on distant hills, the world lay torn, its bonds of trust unravelling thread by fragile thread. When the last shield had fallen and smoke thinned to grey wisps, the survivors found the road ahead divided in two, and on either trail the future waited, blank and breathing. Rulers who had shouted across open borders now felt the quiet tug of shared longing—one future beckoning all to the same new dawn, daring them to gather the scattered pieces, to weave them into a tomorrow where the spark of life might flame brighter still.

Yet, even amid the coalition, secret ambitions and quiet lies hovered like ghosts, ready to crack the fragile peace and feed old grudges. The balance of power dangled above a dark abyss, every treaty strained and every promise weighed. It was here, on the spinning edge of danger, that our heroes found the burden of the choices ahead. A brighter future demanded a toll—losses that the world would remember forever. With the chill of tomorrow's doubt at their throats, they stepped onto a road filled with sharp turns and twisted morals. Each forward push was risky, and the usual maps of right and wrong began to fade in the face of hard choices. As days passed, the tightening snare of secrets and lies closed around them, leaving no space for mistakes and no time for second thoughts. If they stumbled, the cost would drown them. The danger climbed with every heartbeat. Yet, even in the dark crush of trouble, a slender thread of hope unfurled—the stubborn spirit of those who still dared to dream of dawn. The deep centre of human fire, bruised but bright, sliced through the night and drew a narrow, flickering trail toward a second chance.

It was living proof that the hearts of a few had the power to hold back the tide of ruin. Sitting at the edge of night, they marched forward against walls that dared to be called impossible, trusting that even small footsteps could be the keystone of a world that tomorrow would smile upon. For every other face that would follow, they stared down the dark, reeled their deepest beliefs out of yesterday's long shadows, and climbed higher than yesterday's ceiling. The whispers of their choosing would outlive the stars, weaving the first strokes of dawn into the living cloth of tomorrow, where light and victory spun a single, steady flame.

Twilight poured purple and gold over the broken fields, wrapping the ruin in a light that felt borrowed and still too beautiful to refuse. The wind carried the stench of burnt earth and the faint moan of guns, but beneath the weight, a small, defiant ember of possibility held its pulse. From the furnace of battle, a fellowship of once-enemies was sewing itself, stitch by trembling stitch. Leaders who had traded curses now traded vows, standing shoulder to shoulder, their eyes aimed not at the scars around them but at the dreams still breathing within the smoke. Darkness swallowed the last gold, and firelight trembled on their determined faces, casting shadows that dared to spin into laughter.

In that quiet hour, they felt the full force of every choice they had ever made, the road that could never turn back stretching out like an open sea. Duty, honour, and the deepest kind of sacrifice clung to them, and the fate of entire nations rode on the fragile edge of this single moment. One by one, stars blinked into the dark, tiny sparks that whispered of unrealised tomorrows. Every little flash echoed the fire that would not cool in the leaders' chests. The memory of battles fought and the snare of power slipped from their grasp, leaving only the clear, fierce will to bend fate toward something pure and redeeming. Far off, the silhouette of a city climbed the horizon, a jagged wound in the changing sky. It had its scars, still, it throbbed with the same heartbeat that had never surrendered. The leaders remembered that inside its quiet streets, the dreams of ordinary people hushed their fears, singing for a dawn that would glow differently from the past. They felt the weight of every lifted prayer settle on their shoulders. Instead of shrinking, they pressed on, intent to chisel a world where courage outshouted fear and where dark clouds of despair were swept away by a steady dawn. With the last shadows of doubt peeling away, the fragile alliance grasped a shared truth that they had never spoken: the road ahead would twist and tilt with every kind of storm.

Beneath the sky spangled with stars, they pressed together against the chill of night and, despite every wound, discovered the same beating heart that ignores borders and banners. They imagined a cloth of endless tomorrows, stitched with the bright threads of kindness, of listening, of the simple fact that they, like us, are human. That dream was born inside the raging storm of war and kept alive by hands clasped across every divide. The hours passed, still and resolute, for every fellow traveller believed that the hour for change had finally arrived. When dawn's first soft beam broke the night, the light was more than morning's coming; it was the opening chapter of a fresh, shared promise. The sky flared with colours as if the night had kept its word, colouring the world with the hush of a new beginning. The leaders lifted their eyes to the brightening vault and, without flinching, stepped toward the line where earth meets sky, their pledge still ringing, a timeless note in the ever-unfolding story.